PRAISE FOR
Sharyn McCrumb ④
and her
Elizabeth MacPherson
mysteries

"A good deal of suspense...McCrumb writes with a sharp-pointed pen."
—*Los Angeles Times*

"She's Agatha Christie with an attitude; outrageous and engrossing at the same time."
—*Nashville Banner*

"McCrumb's ability to write in a variety of styles—crossing genres, mixing the comic with the serious—makes her one of the most versatile crime authors on the contemporary scene."
—*Booklist*

PAYING THE PIPER

Sharyn McCrumb

BALLANTINE BOOKS · NEW YORK

Copyright © 1988 by Sharyn McCrumb

All rights reserved under International and Pan-American Copyright Conventions. Published in the United States by Ballantine Books, a division of Random House, Inc., New York, and simultaneously in Canada by Random House of Canada Limited, Toronto.

http://www.randomhouse.com

Library of Congress Catalog Card Number: 88-91970

ISBN 0-345-34518-5

Manufactured in the United States of America

First Edition: December 1988

20 19 18 17 16

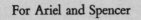

For Ariel and Spencer

ACKNOWLEDGMENTS

The author would like to thank the many experts who were generous with their time and knowledge in helping with the research for this book. Among the most helpful were Lyle Browning, archaeologist for the state of Virginia; Dr. Robert Carman of the Virginia Tech Department of Microbiology; the Cadies—Colin MacPhail and Robin Mitchell—of Edinburgh, who allowed me to use their tour of the Murder Walks of Edinburgh in the narrative; Erich Neumann, for help with information on bagpipes; Dr. Gavin Faulkner, for letting himself be dragged all over Scotland while I researched this book; and Dr. Zach Agioutantis, for his help with computers.

CHAPTER

1

CAMERON

I loaned her eight guidebooks of Scotland, and all the maps that I had, but she only looked at the castles and the pictures of the mountains, bare against the sky.

"Not like our mountains in Virginia," she said. "We have trees. But it's close enough. I guess my MacPherson ancestors must have felt almost at home when they settled there."

They call themselves Scots, these ninth-generation descendants of a MacDonald or a Stewart, and they've no idea what or where the family was in the "old country," but they feel some sort of kinship with Scotland that is half history and half Robert Burns. It isn't the country *I've* come from, though I can't make them see that.

Elizabeth knows more history than I do, but she takes it all personally. Her eyes flash when she talks about the Jacobite Cause, but she mispronounces most of the battles— "Cul-*low*-den," she says. I tell her how to say them correctly, but I can't tell her much about them. It was a long time ago, and nobody minds anymore. I'm a marine biologist, not a historian.

She tells me I don't look Scottish, whatever that means. Lots of people have brown hair and brown eyes. What would she know about it? She's never been there. "I'm a Celt!" she says, the way someone else might say, "I'm a duchess," though I think it's nothing much to be proud of, the way they're carrying on in Belfast. She has the look of them, though, with that mass of black hair and the clear blue eyes of a bomb-throwing Irish saint. She looks at me sometimes, and she knows things I'd never dream of telling her.

She claims no interest in genealogy because she doesn't haunt courthouses or write away for shipping records, but the yearning is there; only she goes about it differently. *"Fash't,"* she'll say. "Do you have that word? Or *clabbered*, or *red the room*?" Sometimes I've heard them, from my grandmother perhaps, and she'll smile as if I've given her something, and say, "From mine, too." She takes me to bluegrass concerts and watches to see if I recognize a song. Often I do, but I don't know if it's because the tune has Celtic roots or if it's because they play country music on Radio Forth. I grew up listening to Jim Reeves and Ernest Tubb as much as she did, but she won't realize that. She thinks that because you can see Edinburgh Castle from our upstairs window at home, somehow we're neighbors of Mary, Queen of Scots, instead of residents of the modern world.

I don't know what she's looking for in the phrases or the mountains or the faces in my photo album, and when she says she loves me, I wonder if she sees me at all.

* * *

PAYING THE PIPER

I don't remember telling her that she could go along when I went back to Scotland to do my summer research. It's as if one moment I was recommending things she might like to see if she ever visited there, and the next, I was writing to Edinburgh University to see if there were any archaeological digs in the Highlands near the island where I'd be doing my seal research. Elizabeth is doing graduate work in forensic anthropology; she studies the bones of something to determine what it was like when it was alive; perhaps this is also her approach to Scottish culture.

There weren't many digs to choose from, and none that were related to her field of study, but one of the replies mentioned that Denny Allan was fielding the requests to join the expedition. A Denny Allan had been in my class at Fettes.

I explained to Elizabeth that the dig offered no pay, no university credit, and was completely out of her field. Still, she insisted that I write to Denny Allan and get her accepted as one of the crew. I pointed out that my own research was solitary, isolated, and time-consuming. Perhaps I could see her on weekends. That was all. She said that weekends were better than nothing. I said I hoped she knew what she was in for. The group would be camping out on the site: *no* modern conveniences, and an uninhabited island with no bridge or ferry service to the mainland and no town nearby. "Don't be fooled by the term *summer*, either," I warned her. "Scotland is cold by your standards, and you may not enjoy tent-dwelling in a rainy climate."

My lament fell on deaf ears, all of it. She is so enchanted at the thought of being "in the Highlands," as she puts it, that all practical considerations are dismissed out of hand. So I wrote to Denny (it turned out he *was* my school chum,

3

after all) and got her a place on the Marchand expedition, studying Celtic standing stones on an island near Skye. I am afraid that she will be disappointed, but she can't say she wasn't told. When I suggested that she might see more museums and castles if she signed up for a bus tour and came over with a group, she wept and accused me of calling her a "tourist," which she said she was not. The MacPherson ancestors, you see. Elizabeth thinks she is "going home."

Dear Cousin Geoffrey,

Yes, I am finally making a trip to Europe, even if I have to "rob graves" (as you so colorfully put it) to get to go.

As a matter of fact, the archaeological expedition I'll be working with is not concerned with unearthing bodies. We're studying megalithic monuments in the Scottish Highlands, in order to determine whether the Celts used Pythagorean geometry in constructing their stone circles. I'll admit that this is not particularly relevant to my graduate work in forensic anthropology (body snatching, to you), but it was the only archaeological dig we could find near where Cameron is doing his summer research. It should work out very nicely: he'll be studying seals, and I'll be measuring standing stones, and we'll get to see each other on weekends.

We're landing in London, so I should get to do some sightseeing on the way to Scotland. Thank you for your travel suggestions, but I don't think I care to visit the alley where Jack the Ripper left his victims, or the eighteenth-century sex club in High Wycombe. Just the usual touristy sites like Oxford and Stratford-on-Avon will suit me fine.

I doubt if I will have either the time or the money to visit you during your vacation in the Greek islands, where you will no doubt be viewed as Dionysus with MasterCard. And if you persist in this quest for the perfect tan, you are going to resemble the cover of a Bible by the time you are fifty!

I'll send you a postcard from Edinburgh (of Burke and Hare, if I can find one), but after that I'll be incommunicado. The dig is on a tiny island with no inhabitants and no mail service. Perhaps we can get together for the family Thanksgiving ordeal and inflict slide shows on one another. Until then—

As ever,
Elizabeth

TRAVELER'S DIARY

You can't sleep on a DC-10. Not this one, anyway, with stewardesses rolling drinks carts up the aisles and making movie announcements and hawking duty-free goods. It's like trying to fly to Britain in a K-Mart. I'm hunched up in my window seat, trying to decide which half of my body I want circulation in and where the Band-Aid sized pillow would do the most good.

"I feel like a squirrel in a coconut!" I hissed to Cameron.

"No. Sorry," he replied. "They only serve those on Caribbean flights."

British humor. I'm still not accustomed to it, even after all these months of knowing Cameron. He seems to be able to take a phrase and turn it inside out, so that I have to think for a minute before I understand the point of the joke. During the year that he has been at the university as a visiting professor, he has been trying to absorb American culture; I, in turn, have spent the year learning him, as if he were a foreign

6

language. Having ancestors who came from Scotland two centuries ago is certainly no help in figuring out a specimen from the present! For the longest time I thought that *dear* was a term of affection, until I began to notice the circumstances in which he used it. "That restaurant is fine, *dear*," when we had to wait an hour for a table. "Next street, I think, *dear*," when I hadn't noticed the sign that said ONE WAY.

Dear means *idiot*.

I still don't know what he would use as a term of affection. It would probably take implements of torture to find out. He said he liked an outfit I was wearing once. And he told me that I was the only woman he could really discuss his work with. Two compliments in a year-long relationship. Whoever said that the British are not demonstrative had a gift for understatement. The only real indication that he likes me is his assumption that I'll always be there, always be free to go out, always want to hear about his experiences at the biology lab. That, and the fact that he eats the potato chips off my plate in restaurants, a sure sign of intimacy. There's more difference between Brits and Americans than a few vocabulary changes—*flat* for *apartment*, and that sort of thing. I don't know how he thinks. Does he simply not show affection, or does he also not feel it?

I wonder what else I'm going to learn about British-American culture while I'm over here.

PEOPLE WHO PRIDE THEMSELVES ON THEIR BRITISH PREP SCHOOL MANNERS SHOULD NOT READ OTHER PEOPLE'S TRAVEL DIARIES WHILE THEY ARE TRYING TO WRITE!

Finally got to sleep (from sheer exhaustion) and woke up to sunlight—at a time my body *knew* was 1:00 A.M.

The cumulus clouds below us look like white outline embroidery seamed on a white quilt. What is that called? Candlewicking? My mother would know. I wonder when we'll see Ireland and if it will really look emerald-green down below. . . .

I must have dozed off. A change in the noise of the airplane engines woke me up, and I looked out the window to see a patchwork of golden fields and green meadows, with little stone houses set all among them. We are much nearer the ground now. Must be coming into Heathrow.

I stand corrected. Gatwick. We are coming into *Gatwick*. And when I find out what *silly git* means, you're going to be in trouble, *Doctor* Dawson, sir.

Caveat, Britannia! Here we come.

"Hmmm," said Elizabeth MacPherson, "the glove compartment in this car is awfully small."

"Glove *box*." Cameron Dawson's correction was automatic. "Small?"

"Yes. I was thinking of crawling into it." She risked a glance out the windshield. "Everybody here is driving on the wrong side of the road, and they must be doing eighty at least."

Cameron smiled. "High speeds are allowed on the M1. You'll be used to it by the time we get to Scotland."

If we get to Scotland, Elizabeth thought, but she tried to look reassured. "It's quite amazing how quickly you got used to British driving again," she remarked. *After that one little incident with the truck as we were leaving the car rental lot*, she added to herself.

"I've only been away for a year," he reminded her. "Look at that car ahead of us. The red one. That's a Vauxhall VX 4/90. You can hear those things two streets away."

"That's nice," Elizabeth said absently. She was scanning the horizon for castles or picturesque villages with cobbled streets, but so far the drive on the motorway from Gatwick had been mostly trees and pastures, looking remarkably like the Virginia landscape they had just left.

"And that white one is a TR6. My cousin had one of those. On a cold day we used to have to stick a fan in the engine to get it started."

"Look!" cried Elizabeth, seeing a flash of purple on the roadside. "Heather!"

Cameron did not spare a glance out the window. "Rosebay willow herb, I expect," he told her. "Heather doesn't grow on roadways in Hampshire, dear."

"It's very pretty, though."

"It's a weed. We had to slave to keep them out of the garden. My father says that during the war willow herb was the first plant to grow in the ruins of a bomb site."

"How lovely!" Elizabeth cried. "Like a condolence card from Nature."

Cameron refused to be drawn into paeans of nature. "That green car is a Moggie Thou—a Morris 1000," he informed her. "My first car was one of those."

Elizabeth sighed. "Cameron, is this your idea of a guided tour of Britain? Identifying all the cars we pass on the motorway?"

He looked puzzled. "Well, you didn't know them, did

you? I haven't seen a Moggie Thou in the States. Thought you'd be interested.''

"Why stop with cars?" asked Elizabeth sarcastically. "See those black-and-white cows in the field? Those are Holsteins.''

Cameron smiled. "Actually, they're not. In this country they're called Friesians.'' Noting the dangerous look in her eyes, he added hastily, "All right! You're the tourist. Just what would you like to see?''

And for the next fifty-six miles she told him.

TRAVELER'S DIARY

Haworth doesn't seem to have changed much since the Brontës' time. Despite the fact that their home has become a shrine for half the English lit majors in the world, the village itself is still a tiny community off a side road in the Yorkshire moors. It wasn't even listed on our map.

"I know the Brontë sisters were notorious recluses," I told Cameron, "but an unlisted *village* is going a bit far!"

He finally located it on a Yorkshire map, in the vicinity of Bradford, and, as out of the way as it was, he agreed to take me there. I had packed a paperback copy of *Wuthering Heights* in my suitcase because I'd hoped we could visit Haworth. There is a modern part of the town down in the valley; you can see it from the road as you drive in, but the village as the sisters knew it is a collection of stone houses on the top of a hill, centering on the church and on the Black Bull Tavern, where Branwell got drunk and claimed to have written Emily's book.

11

I had a real wallow in Haworth, as Cameron so ungallantly phrased it. It was past eight in the evening when we got there (but the sky was as light as afternoon), so the church and the shops were closed, but I insisted on spending an hour in the churchyard, looking for the Brontë graves. (That was a waste of time. When we went into the church the next morning, we discovered the plaque that said the family was buried in a crypt inside the church. There are no graves, per se. So much for a private word with Emily.) Then, as the sun was setting, I hauled Cameron off to the moors, sat on a hill in the white heather, and read my favorite passages from *Wuthering Heights:*

> ". . . I was only going to say that heaven did not seem to be my home; and I broke my heart with weeping to come back to earth; and the angels were so angry that they flung me out, into the middle of the heath on the top of Wuthering Heights, where I woke sobbing for joy . . ."

Cameron was looking somewhat restive, since his knowledge of British literature equals my knowledge of manatee breeding. I ignored the glazed look in his eyes and kept reading. It was so beautiful, to be out on the actual moor on which Emily used to wander, in the gathering twilight . . . no one within miles of us. It could have done with a few trees, but it was still lovely. Miles and miles of dark green hills outlined in stone walls, and nothing of the twentieth century in sight.

In an effort to capture Cameron's flagging attention (which was probably focused on car repair), I began to explain the plot of the novel, and that the passage I was reading explained Catherine's love for Heathcliff. Very romantic, I thought, hoping that he'd come and sit by me. No such luck.

". . . He does not know what being in love is?"
"I see no reason that he should not know, as well as you," I returned; "and if *you* are his choice, he'll be the most unfortunate creature that ever was born! As soon as you become Mrs. Linton, he loses friend, and love, and all! Have you considered how you'll bear the separation, and how he'll bear to be quite deserted in the world? Because, Miss Catherine—"
"He quite deserted! We separated!" she exclaimed, with an accent of indignation. "Who is to separate us, pray? They'll meet the fate of Milo . . ."

My voice trailed off, and I wouldn't look at Cameron. As many times as I'd read *Wuthering Heights*, I hadn't seen that. Of course, it wouldn't have registered before. I had been trying not to think about my own Milo and all the awkwardness that had occurred when I came back from the Highland Games, having met Cameron, and ended the "understanding" we'd had for a couple of years.

Milo had taken it well. "I'm a forensic anthropologist," he kept saying. "I don't understand live people." But I knew he was hurt, and the guilt was like a pebble in my shoe. I couldn't quite shake it. I really did feel caught between Linton and Heathcliff—only I wasn't sure which was which.

Cameron must have seen me blush and guessed what word had thrown me, but British reserve does not allow him to discuss such matters. "Very nice book," he observed politely. "Now, which one of the Brontë sisters was it who wrote *Pride and Prejudice*?"

By the time I stopped laughing, the mood had passed and

so had the light, so we went down the hill and followed the path back to the village for dinner at the Black Bull Tavern, where Branwell Brontë drank himself to death—perhaps from a broken heart.

CHAPTER

2

The drive from London to Edinburgh had been a clash of tourism, compounded of Elizabeth's romantic Britain and Cameron's more prosaic stopping points. Oxford University and the Donnington Park car museum; the Brontës' village and Harry Ramsden's famous fish restaurant; the Border Abbeys and the Dewsbury market (cheap tools, tape recorders, and electronics parts). They tolerated each other's obsessions with affectionate good humor, but with very little real interest.

They reached Edinburgh on a rainy Friday evening—in time for tea, a salmon salad prepared by Cameron's mother in honor of the American visitor who might turn out to be someone "significant." Elizabeth smiled prettily and tried not to feel like Wallis Simpson.

Cameron's younger brother Ian had come home from the University of Strathclyde for the weekend, and he spent a good bit of time trying to convince Elizabeth to attend the

Commonwealth Games. The fact that the Queen might be there was an alluring prospect, but in the end Elizabeth decided that even flesh-and-blood royalty could not tempt her into sitting through a "special Olympics for British subjects," as she put it.

"Elizabeth doesn't like anything that hasn't been dead a hundred years," Cameron told his brother.

"Well, that explains her attraction to you." Ian smirked.

During the ensuing pillow fight, Elizabeth helped Margaret Dawson with the washing up.

The next morning was cloudy, but not actually raining—a typical British summer day, Elizabeth had learned. Cameron had promised her a full day's tour of the city, but he explained that he had a few errands to attend to first, and Elizabeth had gamely agreed to accompany him.

"We'll get to the castle, I promise you. I shouldn't be much longer here. What time is your meeting this afternoon?"

"Three o'clock," said Elizabeth, consulting her watch. "I don't suppose we'll have time for the museum as well?"

No reply was forthcoming. By that time the salesman had unearthed another catalogue, and he and Cameron were rooting through it happily, talking about master cylinders and oil seals.

Oil seals. That was what threw her. When Cameron, the marine biologist, had announced that he wanted to consult Halfords about oil seals, before they went sightseeing, she had assumed it had to do with his research, and naturally she had agreed. Halfords, she thought, must be some sort of aquarium or research station on the Firth of Forth, and she looked forward to watching the seals cavorting about in the water, or, failing that, she could at least view the other exhibits while Cameron made his inquiries.

She spent the first few minutes of the drive enjoying the scenery and studying the houses and gardens, so that they were several miles along before she brought up the subject of the trip. "Is this a new research project, then?"

"What?" said Cameron.

"This Halfords trip. Are you studying the effects of North Sea oil drilling on the seals?"

Cameron had found that so amusing that he had repeated it to the clerk, the cashier, and to two other customers in Halfords—which turned out to be an auto-parts store. After his performance on the M1, she should have known; but somehow she hadn't thought of British men as being car-crazed. Horses, perhaps. That would have fit in with her God-is-an-Englishman view of the species, but somehow an obsession with batteries and spark plugs lacked the aura of romance that she associated with tweeds and spaniels.

She didn't complain, though. She sat down at the catalogue table in the corner and wrote postcards while Cameron blethered on about his car troubles. Perhaps she had romanticized him a bit, she thought. "Built him a soul," as Dorothy Parker had phrased it. But after all, it did seem to fit rather nicely. And even carburetors had a certain charm when they were discussed in a cultured Scottish accent.

Elizabeth smiled sweetly at Halfords in general. Everything was romantic in Britain.

CHAPTER

3

The National Museum of Antiquities, on Edinburgh's Queen Street, across from Scotland's National Portrait Gallery, was to be the setting for the first meeting of the archaeologists working on the Banrigh project. The museum's principal exhibit at the moment was "I Am Come Home," a tribute to Charles Edward Stuart that featured some of the Bonnie Prince's own personal possessions, including his silver mess kit for "roughing it." With the possible exception of the American members of the expedition, everyone would give that room a miss in favor of the more ancient relics of Scotland.

Derek Marchand had arrived early for the dig's organizational meeting because he believed in being punctual. After he had checked out the meeting room upstairs, he had gone back to the first floor of the museum to have a look around while he organized his thoughts.

The St. Ninian's Isle treasure was popular, as usual. Crowds of people were milling about the glass cases looking at the silver bowls and penannular Pictish brooches that had been found on Shetland in the 1950s. A professor from Aberdeen University had been excavating on the small island to locate and plan the medieval church that had once stood there. A schoolboy volunteer on the dig had turned over a broken stone in what had been the nave of the church and had found the larchwood box containing treasure: twenty-eight decorated silver objects—and the jawbone of a porpoise. No doubt the Picts had hidden their valuables beneath the church floor during a Viking raid and had never reclaimed the box.

Marchand smiled. This was most people's idea of archaeology: finding heavily carved silver jewelry stashed away in the earth. He had been a schoolboy himself when Howard Carter found even gaudier treasure in the grave of Tutankhamen in Egypt. Perhaps that story had awakened his own passion for archaeology. If so, he had long outgrown such romantic notions. Now, as a man of seventy, choosing archaeology as the avocation of his retirement, he preferred knowledge to trinkets. A few handfuls of wood ash or a trowel of bone fragments could offer more information than a trunkful of silver-gilt brooches. He was no longer interested in treasure troves.

Marchand bent over a case containing stone axes and flint microliths. The tools of ancient Britain still fascinated him, and made him feel a kinship with those early engineers, perhaps more so than with their modern counterparts. Having served with the Royal Corps of Engineers in World War II, Marchand knew what it meant to accommodate your structures to nature, just as the old ones did. These days young civil engineers had the money and the technology to change the environment to suit their needs: level the mountain, divert the river. They hadn't done it that way in Greece in 1943. The war had deprived them of the luxury of time and technology. They'd had three days to build a bridge, and they had to put it where nature would permit. Yes, he understood the Celts: using makeshift tools to negotiate a truce with the elements. He admired them for it.

He rather thought he might resemble one of the ancient Celts. He was just over five feet seven but still fit, and with a mane of silvery hair, a bit thin on top. He didn't suppose many of them had lived as long as he had; seventy was nearly double the life expectancy in prehistoric Britain. Still, he felt it would have been a good time to live. He could think of few things in the twentieth century that he would miss. Certainly not telephones, automobiles, or television sets. He was pleased that the dig site would have none of those modern inconveniences. Their absence would make him feel closer to the ancient builders; perhaps it would bring them luck.

Because the Scottish Museum had been closer to Buckingham Terrace than he'd expected, Owen Gilchrist was twenty minutes early for the organizational meeting of the Banrigh dig. If he hadn't been carrying camera equipment, he would have walked instead of taking a cab, but he had wanted to photograph the house. Owen wished he'd had the nerve to go up and knock on the door, but the place was obviously a private home, and perhaps its occupants didn't even know that a murder had been committed there fifty years ago. Owen knew—because his hobby was murder.

In 1926 the sandstone row house had been home to John Donald Merrett, an Edinburgh University student who had shot and killed his mother—one of the few matricides ever recorded in Scotland. The façade of the house seemed unchanged from

20

the photographs Owen had seen in his crime books. He wondered about the interior, but he was too shy to seek admittance.

The infamous Merrett house was not listed in any of the cheery paperback guidebooks Owen had purchased back in Ohio to prepare for his summer in Scotland; all of them recommended the conventional fare for visitor: the castle, the Royal Mile, and the art gallery. Owen's taste in tourism was quite different, but fortunately he was well versed in his specialty and needed no assistance other than the city maps provided by less sanguine guidebook writers.

Owen had spent the three days before the start of the dig in an absolute orgy of crime—all vicariously experienced, that is. He had paid his respects to the skeleton of Burke the Body Snatcher, on display at the Royal College of Surgeons, and on a side trip to Sir Walter Scott's home at Abbotsford he insisted upon seeing the bit of Burke's tanned flesh that Scott supposedly kept in a stamp box. (The grandmotherly guide had disavowed all knowledge of such a barbarity in strangled tones suggesting that she wouldn't mind having Owen similarly displayed with a placard reading: TOURISTUS AMERICANUS.)

He had had lunch in Deacon Brodie's Tavern, a pub named after the original model for Stevenson's *Dr. Jekyll and Mr. Hyde*, and he had toured Edinburgh's famous old prison, the Tollbooth, happily reminiscing about the Porteous Riot and the *Heart of Midlothian* executions.

Owen Gilchrist knew that his hobby was a bit unusual, but he did not consider himself at all strange. Scores of people his age and younger went to "dead teenager" movies, sitting through an evening of axe murders or chainsaw massacres in living color, and no one seemed to worry about *their* mental health. He, by contrast, simply combined the adolescent fas-

21

cination with gore with an interest in history; to him the stories were the more exciting for being true.

Owen Gilchrist didn't encounter much excitement in the ordinary course of his life. Owen, who had been accused of being born middle-aged, was having a sedate time at college, with none of the wild parties and romantic escapades experienced by college students in films. He was a pudgy, bespectacled teddy bear to whom sex was still a branch of philosophy, and his major in anthropology suggested an interest in people that was as impersonal in his private life as it was in his course work. His acquaintances considered him timid and a trifle immature, and so he was; but he could be quite merciless when tracking a serial killer through the pages of a true-crime biography. He had studied all the major murderers of the twentieth century, and he would go on about "Ted" or "Ian and Myra" as if they were his dearest friends. Perhaps they were. Certainly they provided him with more entertainment and less hassle than those he met in his everyday existence. Sometimes he imagined the jock types in his dorm being dismembered by a crazed psychopath, or an unattainable sorority member bound, gagged, and terrified in a lantern-lit cellar, awaiting the pleasure of Owen-the-Ripper. But he wouldn't actually do it "in real life"; dear me, no. It was a harmless form of fantasy; Owen was always unfailingly polite to his college classmates. He must have lost a dozen pens a month because he was too shy to ask for the return of them. His fantasies, though, were his own business.

He hoped that the archaeological dig would provide a bit of ghoulish excitement. Surely they would find a few skeletons in the course of the excavation. Owen had read about the bog people, a prehistoric Norse tribe that had left ritually throttled sacrifices in tannin bogs, so perfectly preserved by the natural acids that, twenty centuries later, they were mistaken for recent murder victims. If there were any bogs on the isle of Banrigh, Owen would certainly search them. If not, perhaps the standing stones would yield a few bony offerings to the sun god; he heard of similar finds at Stonehenge in the south.

As inoffensive as Owen was, he had recently adopted one antisocial habit that he planned to perfect during the course of the dig. He hoped no one would object, but he vowed to make no concessions on this point to his fellow diggers. Owen had every intention of continuing his self-taught bagpipe lessons.

Gitte Dankert looked at her watch for the third time in as many minutes. "Please finish your salad, Alasdair," she urged. "You are going to make us late for the meeting."

Her companion, interrupted in a tale about his anatomy lecturer, scowled and set down his fork. "Don't be so bloody punctual! I suppose the trains run on time in Denmark?"

"We always try to arrive on schedule for a meeting," Gitte said seriously.

"Don't worry about it. I'm the medical man for the expedition, so I needn't follow all the petty little rules set down for the ditchdiggers."

"But, Alasdair, I'm one of those ditchdiggers," she said softly.

"Nonsense! You're with me. Don't take offense, love." He yanked one strand of her mousy fringe, and then he went back to his salad, spearing forkfuls of bean sprouts and nuts in the same leisurely fashion as before.

Gitte sighed, resigning herself to being late for the meeting. If she continued to press the point, they would only be that much later. She knew these moods of Alasdair's. He could be quite charming when he wanted, but his opinion of himself was very high. Her flat-mates joked that he acted as if M.D. stood for *medical deity*, and they warned her that if he was this difficult as a third-year student, he would only become worse as he came closer to qualifying.

Gitte suspected that they were right, but she didn't seem to be able to help herself. When Alasdair was rude to everyone else but nice to her, she felt very special and privileged, and when he was brusque with her, it made her try all the harder to win his approval. She supposed she loved him—the fact that he was not particularly good-looking or passionate made her feel virtuous in her affection. Surely it could not be mere animal magnetism if he were so drab and serious; surely only true love would kindle with so little fuel. She wondered at times how he felt about her. She was not very pretty, with her dull brown hair and lashless green eyes, but she was small and thin and twenty-two, which counted for beauty in the everyday world. There was always an offer or two to buy her a shandy at the pub, and Alasdair seemed gratified by that, as if being her escort allowed him pride of ownership. But she wondered if that attractiveness counted enough—for a serious relationship, that is. "Buy British" seemed to apply to more than manufactured goods; often she felt that being a Dane made her somehow "not quite the article," a favorite expression of Alasdair's. Perhaps it explained the drink offers as well. Danes seemed to have earned a reputation for sexual liberation that Gitte did not live up to at all, but fortunately Alasdair did not seem to mind her shyness. He was a bit of a prude himself.

She had never met his family. He said he was estranged from them, but she wondered if that could be an excuse. Still, she knew that he wasn't seeing anyone else, and she supposed that being taken for granted could be interpreted as a kind of devotion.

British men were quite undemonstrative, and she thought that perhaps the language barrier could keep her from understanding the nuances of their relationship. It is one thing to be able to understand university courses taught in English, but quite another to pick up the shades of meaning in private life. Of course, Alasdair did not speak Danish, except for the simplest and most anglicized words, like *farvel*, for goodbye. He assumed that she would accommodate him—at great advantage to herself, he thought—by learning perfect English.

Sometimes Gitte bristled at her lover's condescending attitude toward her heritage, but mostly she didn't. If he thought himself such an altogether superior person, perhaps it was true, and in that case she was very lucky to have him.

She was pleased that he had asked her to go along on the archaeological dig. He would have gone without her, of course, and he hadn't consulted her about it beforehand, but at least he had permitted her to accompany him. She told herself that Alasdair was a lonely and troubled person, and that if only she loved him enough, all would be well.

Tom Leath rather liked Edinburgh, It was less crowded and noisy than his usual haunts in a suburb of London. He liked the look of the castle perched there over everything, never letting you forget for a moment that you were treading on history at every turn. He thought he might like to get assigned to a dig there sometime, perhaps more excavations of the Roman fort at Cramond. It was a yacht basin now, quite a picturesque village of whitewashed stone houses and a bit of park overlooking the River Almond and the Firth of Forth. Trust the Romans to take the best property around.

Of course, the night life in Edinburgh was nil—not only compared to London; probably compared to downtown Brighton. What did you bloody do in Edinburgh after dark if you were under forty and on your own?

It would be good practice for the Isle of Banrigh, though. Dead deserted, that was, and not even any electricity for the telly. He'd bought a few bottles of moderately priced Scotch to take over in his rucksack; perhaps some of the other diggers would be sociable types, and they could have a camp fire after work and pass round the old bottle. He expected it to be cold and drizzling on Banrigh, summer or not; the Scottish islands were all the same, climates like basements. Leath thought, not for the first time, that being a specialist in Celtic culture could have its drawbacks. Had he specialized in Greek archaeology, he could be lounging on Delos right now, acquiring a healthy tan along with the potsherds.

Marchand should be all right as head of the expedition. He was ex-army. He'd be all right in terms of leniency, that is, toward the odd bit of drinking or high spirits. Leath wasn't so sure about his being all right in terms of archaeology, though. After all, the man was an engineer, and he wasn't much of an expert on Celtic culture in general—just that one bee in his bonnet about the standing stones.

Leath thought of Heinrich Schliemann, who troweled through half a dozen cities and threw the remains of Troy on the scrap heap because he thought that it should be a few meters deeper in the earth. Archaeology had tried to become more of a science since those days, but there were still enough contract archaeologists around to create problems. He'd heard of one extraordinary fellow in Wyoming in the United States who used the local Indian ruins to provide a sort of dude ranch for scholarly minded tourists. He had built a dormitory and conference center, and he charged people hefty sums to go and paw about in the foothills, pretending to be archaeologists. Probably made a fortune; Leath hoped there hadn't been anything there for him to destroy. If the world was lucky, the bugger was a complete crook who seeded the earth with newly made arrowheads before each new wave of diggers.

Leath didn't suppose that Marchand was as complete an idiot as that. After all, he had managed to get Aberdeen University to sponsor him, and they had instructed him to appoint a Celtic culture person as advisor to the expedition. That was Leath. At twenty-nine, he had a degree in archaeology from Manchester and a dozen years' experience on excavations throughout England, Wales, and Brittany. The Banrigh dig would be his first in Scotland, but he didn't expect to see too many differences in the Celtic remains. They probably wouldn't be finding much, anyway, since all the old bampot wanted to do was measure stone circles and to prove his engineering theory. Leath didn't think Marchand could do much damage under those circumstances; in fact, he intended to make damn sure he didn't.

Elizabeth MacPherson always visited a museum gift shop before she went round to see the exhibits. That way she didn't have to wonder about what gifts and postcards there would be to choose from, and there was no danger of losing track of time in an interesting exhibit and not having the opportunity to browse in the gift shop before it closed.

Since only twenty minutes remained before the archaeological meeting, Elizabeth decided to spend it selecting postcards—while Cameron talked to Denny Allan, who had also come for the meeting. Or rather, she gave a convincing imitation of someone engrossed in choosing postcards; actually she was maintaining a careful surveillance of the meeting between Cameron and his old friend. They made an unlikely pair, she thought. Cameron was tall and serious and rather patrician-looking, and Denny could have modeled for a leprechaun poster. Watching them converse reminded her of a terrier racing and barking around a Great Dane. She had wondered a bit what Cameron would say about her, but he didn't seem to have much chance of getting a word in edgewise.

Denny finally paused for breath after a long account of his troubles with the city street improvement department. He then asked, "So, what's it like in the States, Cameron?"

"Well, they don't all drive like the Dukes of Hazzard," Cameron replied. "Some of the back roads are pretty primitive, though. I nearly got a rock through my windshield last month."

"Windshield? Listen to yourself talking like them already! I suppose you say *gas* now, instead of *petrol*?"

"So would you if you wanted anybody to understand you!" Cameron retorted. He was already fed up with remarks about his accent, or the loss thereof. The unkindest cut of all had come in Bradford when a woman who had been chatting with Elizabeth asked where they were headed. When Cameron told her Edinburgh, she had assured him he'd love the city, and began to suggest places for him to visit. Cameron assumed his frostiest air of dignity and snapped, "I was *borrn* there!" He had been further annoyed when Elizabeth suggested that he should have heeded the woman's suggestions, because, in fact, he never had visited the Tollbooth, the Museum of Childhood, or John Knox's house.

Deciding to change the subject before he lost his temper, Cameron thanked Denny for choosing Elizabeth to join the expedition.

Denny grinned. "No problem! I'd have done it on vulgar curiosity alone. You could have knocked me over with a feather when I got your card. Imagine stuffy old Dawson the seal-man wanting his lady friend over for the summer!"

Cameron didn't like the way this conversation was going, either. He noticed that Elizabeth had been examining the same four postcards for a considerable amount of time without turning the rack. "Yes, well, I'm sure she'll be an asset to the dig. She's quite knowledgeable about bones." Seeing the snappy retort forming on Denny's lips, he added hastily, "Dead people, I mean. Identifying remains. You know—skulls!"

"Yes, but we aren't supposed to find any, Cameron. We're just measuring monoliths. Still, there's always the off chance, and she'd be a useful person to have around. Wish I could think of a way to bring one of my birds along. I take it we'll be seeing a lot of you these next few weeks as well?"

Cameron shrugged. "A fair amount. I'll be monitoring a seal herd from Canna, and I'll have a skiff. I expect I'll come over to see you once a week if the weather holds."

"Well, don't expect too much privacy. It's a small island." Still grinning, Denny motioned for Elizabeth to join them. "I hear you're an anthropology student," he remarked. "Do you know what a seal-man is?"

Elizabeth smiled. "A selkie? Only from the Joan Baez recording. 'I am a man upon the land; I am a selkie on the sea.'"

29

They are magic seal-people who take mortal form on dry land to—umm—to mate with human maidens.''

"Right. On the islands we'll be going to, they called them the *Raoine*. The legends are very similar. Just remember that unless you take away their skin, they always go back to their own kind eventually."

Elizabeth nodded. "I know," she said, looking at Cameron. "It's never quite safe to love a seal-man."

CHAPTER

4

CAMERON

Elizabeth is upstairs in her archaeology meeting, and I am left to wander about in the museum until she is finished. I feel as though I have been wandering about in a museum all these past ten days. Elizabeth seems to see Britain the way the rest of us see the stars: not as they are now, but as they were centuries ago when their light first shone out into space. When we look up into the sky, we see old light; and when she looks out the windscreen of our rental car, she sees the high road to Caledonia, I think. Elizabeth slept through the factories and the concrete mushroom cooling towers of the Midlands, to wake up in a cobblestoned village in Yorkshire, only a century too late for tea at the vicarage.

She picked white heather in the twilight on Haworth Moor and quoted lines on star-crossed lovers from *Wuthering Heights*: "Whatever our souls are made of, his and mine are the same . . ." But it seemed to me that another line on the page suited us more: ". . . as different as a moonbeam from

31

lightning, or frost from fire.'' When she says she loves me,
I can almost guess what she means. It isn't the steady cottage-
and-children, tea-in-front-of-the-telly sort of affection she's
after, but some sort of mythic ritual, fueled by the differences
between us: accent and culture. When I speak, she hears not
only my words, but also the sounds of Byron and Walter
Scott and, for all I know, the Bonnie Prince himself, and I
wonder just which of us it is that she loves, and which myth
she will finally choose for us.

The enchantment followed us into the Eildon Hills of the
Borders. She recognized the name from her folklore studies:
it was home to Thomas the Rhymer. About eight centuries
ago, as near as I could make out. Elizabeth told me the legend, looking out across the sweep of low green hills unchanged by the centuries. She never looked at the lorries
rumbling past us up the motorway.

Thomas of Ercildoune, she said (mispronouncing it), was
an ordinary Scottish villager sitting in the forest one day,
when the Queen of Elfland rode up on her white horse and
carried him off to the fairy kingdom. A mysterious foreign
woman and an ordinary Scot . . . I could see where this was
going . . . they rode through swirling mists and crossed a
stream filled with all the blood that is shed on earth, and at
last in Elfland she gave him an apple that granted him the
gift of prophecy. He left her after seven years to return to his
home in Ercildoune, but years later, while Thomas was at-
tending a village feast, two white deer appeared at the edge
of the forest, and he announced that they had come for him.
Off he went and was never seen again. Back to the Queen of
Elfland—to stay in *her* country forever after.

She stole a glance at me when she finished the story. "Does his village still exist?" she asked. "Ercildoune?"

"Earlston," I corrected her. "Oh, yes. The A68 goes right through it."

Derek Marchand hunched over the conference table and inspected his troops. "Only six?" he said, with a puzzled glance at Denny Allan.

"Yes, well, there is one more," Denny told him. "Callum Farthing will be along on the dig, but he couldn't make the meeting. Prior appointment of some sort. He's a good fellow, though. Archaeology student from Inverness."

Marchand looked as if he wanted to comment further on this early dereliction of duty, but he merely nodded. "Right, then, I'll begin. As you must know by now, I am Derek Marchand, and I'll be heading up this investigation, but the dig is actually financed by a grant from Aberdeen University. That is who will be paying your princely salaries."

Sour smiles from the diggers. Archaeology pays less than lemonade stands.

"I shall outline the purpose to you first, and then we'll get acquainted and go into the logistics of everything."

Elizabeth wrote down *logistics* on her notepad, changing the last *s* to a drawing of a seal.

"As you know, chambered tombs and long cairns are a part of Celtic culture found in much of western Europe, but only in Britain do we find the circular earthworks called *henge monuments*; that is, a deep ditch, a concentric outer bank, and entrance causeways through the ditch and bank." Marchand held up a diagram of a site resembling Stonehenge.

"We are just beginning to examine this sort of monument. The Banrigh site, where we shall be working, is a great stone circle. You may think of it as a prehistoric Westminster Abbey, if you like. Actually we know very little about them: how they were built, or why."

Tom Leath smiled at this. *You know less about them than that,* he thought. *If we learn anything about the culture, it will be in spite of you.*

"Our purpose in the present phase of the dig is to attempt to discover the unit of measurement used by these ancient engineers. We will mark off the circle and measure it to see whether—as Alexander Thom has claimed—a megalithic yard was used to determine distances within the stone circle."

"What about the island?" asked Alasdair McEwan in a bored voice.

"Banrigh is a rather remote little island in the Hebrides. There were a few farms and a small village there until early in this century, but the inhabitants are long since gone."

Elizabeth looked up from her notes. "We won't be staying in tents, will we?"

Marchand smiled. "I can tell by that American accent of yours that you're not accustomed to a Scottish summer," he said playfully.

Elizabeth shivered. "Has there ever been one?"

Denny laughed. "Actually, there is some sort of structure on Banrigh, isn't there?"

Marchand nodded. "During the war, the island was used as a weather station for the North Atlantic fleets, and an army Nissen hut used by those chaps is still standing. It's a bit rusty, and the electricity's long gone, but it will serve to keep the rain off our backs."

34

Owen Gilchrist frowned. "The island is deserted?"

"Another American accent," Marchand remarked. "Young man, we will be alone on Banrigh, but we will hardly be castaways. We will have a radio with us for emergency communications, and a marine biologist who will be working on an island several miles away has kindly offered to come in once a week and to bring in supplies."

Elizabeth wondered if she were blushing at this oblique reference to Cameron.

Owen did not look reassured. "But suppose one of us gets hurt?"

"That, I think, will be my concern," said Alasdair with a condescending smile. "Archaeology is only my hobby. I'm a medical student at Edinburgh University."

"And very kind of you to come along and look after us," said Marchand heartily.

Tom Leath winced. He hoped the self-appointed doctor wouldn't turn out to be a prima donna. The expedition was too small to carry any dead weight in the crew.

"Well, then, that seems settled. Is there anything else to be said before I get on to the technical part of our briefing?"

Owen Gilchrist beamed across the table at his newfound comrades. "Would anyone like to have dinner with a vampire?"

"You should have seen their faces!" Elizabeth grinned. "They must have thought he was completely crazy!"

"Don't be too sure he isn't," Denny added. "But it does sound like a lovely evening, Cameron. Why don't we all go?"

With counterpoint interjections Denny and Elizabeth explained Owen's invitation to experience one of Edinburgh's most unusual tourist attractions. First came dinner at nine at The Witchery, an elegant restaurant in an old building on the Royal Mile, just a few yards from the entrance to Edinburgh Castle. Owen had been so sure of everyone's enthusiasm that he had booked two tables.

"And he would be awfully hurt if he had to cancel both of them," Elizabeth said.

Cameron looked suspicious. "Who else is going?"

Denny grinned. "Marchand and his assistant both pleaded prior engagements. It's probably true."

"And I think the Danish girl wanted to come, but her doctor-boyfriend is a prig." Elizabeth sniffed. "He said he had some work to do before he could leave for the dig, and that the least Gitte could do for him would be to get his laundry ready and pack for him."

"His bedside manner seems less than promising," Denny agreed.

"I take it that we have already agreed to go in order to spare young Owen's feelings?" Cameron asked wearily.

"Not at all," said Elizabeth. "We have agreed to go because I wouldn't miss it for the world!"

"Dinner, she means," Cameron remarked to Denny.

Elizabeth put out her tongue at him. "That wasn't what I was talking about. I want to see the vampire!"

"Steady on!" said Cameron. "What vampire?"

"It's a deceased highwayman, actually," Denny said. "Two young businessmen have come up with a splendid innovation in guided tours. They're leading the tourists all around the so-called Murder Walks of Edinburgh in an after-dark excursion."

"Just the evening for a forensic anthropologist, I suppose?" Cameron asked. "Sort of a busman's holiday, Elizabeth?"

Elizabeth nodded. "Not to mention all the favors you owe me for the auto-parts stores I've suffered through."

"And this is how you want to spend your last evening in civilization? Trailing around after a vampire? You're sure?"

Elizabeth grinned. "A-positive!"

CHAPTER

5

Elizabeth loved The Witchery. As soon as she entered the candlelit restaurant, with its white stone walls and its Halloween decor, she succumbed to an attack of folklore expertise and proceeded to wander around the room examining all the wall decorations and occult graffiti and explaining their significance to Cameron, Denny, and Owen.

"The Pentagram, of course, is a symbol of protection. One is supposed to stand inside it when—"

Denny grinned. "Let's order dinner—and hope she doesn't talk with her mouth full."

"Anthropology major," Cameron said apologetically to the waitress, as he led Elizabeth away from the stuffed goat's head and back to their table. "What would you like for dinner, dear? Eye of newt? Toe of frog?"

"This is a neat place!" Owen exclaimed. "I don't know much about medieval Scotland, though. Except for Sawney Bean."

Cameron and Denny exchanged blank looks.

"You've never heard of Sawney Bean?" Owen asked incredulously. "But you're from Scotland!"

Cameron shrugged. "He didn't write seal monographs."

"No, he was a cannibal."

"And is he coming to dinner tonight as well?" Denny asked politely.

While the waitress took their orders for venison and steak with peppercorns, Owen Gilchrist was silent, his sense of dignity struggling with his desire to show off. The latter won.

Finally, staring into the candle flame for inspiration, he began in a ghost-story whisper. "Sawney Bean lived on the coast of Ayrshire in the fifteenth century. Travelers in that part of Scotland kept disappearing. They hanged an innkeeper, thinking he had been killing off his guests, but the disappearances kept on. Finally, a traveler got away!"

Elizabeth ignored Cameron's stern look. It meant either "What an odd lot you archaeologists are!" or "What an odd lot you Americans are!" She didn't like shouldering responsibility for either group. After all, Cameron's friends wouldn't win any prizes, either. They talked forever about seal research and left dinner parties early to return home and feed their ferrets. For spite she gave Owen her most encouraging smile.

Owen's face glowed in the candlelight as he described the wounded traveler making his way to the nearest town and reporting being attacked by a band of savages. A search party was formed to scour the countryside. "They found nothing," Owen said dramatically. "Until they looked in a cave that could only be entered at low tide."

The waitress looked a bit disconcerted as she set the salad

plates in front of them, but Owen was too deep in his recitation to notice. "When they entered the cave, they found Sawney, his wife, and a tribe of their children and grandchildren-by-incest, living among piles of stolen gold and jewels. Hanging from the roof of the cave were human arms and legs—like a smokehouse!"

Denny set down his fork. "Well, that's done it for dinner." He sighed.

"What happened to them?" asked Elizabeth.

"They were taken back to Edinburgh and burned at the stake," Owen said. "Even in the fifteenth century they were considered subhuman savages."

"Whereas burning them in public was mature and civilized behavior," Elizabeth said sweetly. She returned Cameron's stern stare, hoping that he would feel a collective responsibility for Scots of all eras, but it did not work. Cameron was not checking Sawney Bean into his emotional baggage.

"You're an unusual sort of tourist," Denny remarked. "Even for an American. Most of them seem to have a Robert Burns fixation."

"Or Macbeth," Cameron grunted.

Owen flushed. "Murder is sort of a hobby of mine," he mumbled. "I'm not a kook or anything. I just like scary stories that happen to be true. The tour tonight should be great!"

Cameron smiled faintly. "I've always thought of Edinburgh as a sleepy old lady. I'm sure this will provide a new perspective."

Owen grinned. "She may be sleepy now, but she's had quite a past!"

* * *

For the rest of dinner the conversation proceeded along tamer lines. The three archaeologists discussed Marchand's lecture and details of the Banrigh dig. Owen was stunned to learn that neither of the two native Scots could help him at all in his efforts to learn to play bagpipes. Denny announced that he preferred the banjo, and Cameron disavowed all knowledge of music. Elizabeth said carefully that she didn't think it was necessary to practice too much in order to become a good player.

Cameron explained his seal migration project to Owen, who countered with his own marine biology story—that of a shark in Australia who vomited up the tatooed arm of a murder victim, thus enabling police to solve the case.

Just as they were finishing their coffee, a sudden hush fell upon the restaurant as a tall young man in a vampire cloak swept into the room. His face was covered with white stage makeup, and his dark hair was slicked down like paint on a porcelain doll. One by one, the Witchery guests who had signed up for the tour left their tables to form a cluster around their strange guide. When everyone was ready, he led the gaggle of tourists out into the twilight and up the cobbled street to the castle esplanade.

In the gathering darkness the street seemed old and empty, hardly part of the present century at all. The group shivered with anticipation as they circled around the shadow man.

"My name is Adam Lyal," the guide said in a smooth Edinburgh accent. "Deceased," he added with a grin.

The crowd of tourists tittered nervously. The night air was chilly, and the deepening shadows heightened the effect of the ghoul makeup.

"I was a highwayman here in Edinburgh in the eighteenth century. Got hanged for it, too. But the devil has allowed me to come back to earth on the condition that I guide the living along the Murder Walks of Edinburgh's dark history. Every night I take groups like this one up and down the closes, searching out the darkest corners of Auld Reekie's grimy past."

"Will we be visiting the Merrett house?" someone called out.

Adam Lyal (deceased) frowned. "No, he's not on our tour," he answered. "It would be a considerable departure to get to his house. He's small potatoes anyway. Compared to some of us," he added menacingly.

At the mention of his latest crime obsession—by someone other than himself—Owen became instantly alert. "Another crime buff!" he whispered to Elizabeth. "I'll be back."

As the tour wound its way farther up the hill into the shadow of the castle to the spot at the barricade where the witches had once been executed, Owen threaded his way through the crowd and finally reached the side of the man who'd asked the question: a tall, stocky Englishman in a green anorak.

"I visited the Merrett house this afternoon," Owen offered as an opening gambit. "I don't think the people know it's a crime scene."

The older man nodded. "Not very dramatic looking, is it? Still, a black and white shot in the right light might set it off."

"Are you interested in murders?" whispered Owen, trying to appear casual.

"Well, it's a living." The man smiled, turning his attention back to the guide.

The young soldier on guard at the castle entrance had been listening to Adam Lyal's account of the witch-burning. "Looks like they missed a few," he remarked in tones suggesting that the banter was a nightly occurrence.

The deceased highwayman was ready with a reply. "And this young man," he said, pointing to the soldier, "will have to stay up here a-aaall night . . . a-aaall alo-oone."

"Right. Well, I'll stock up on holy water," the guard called out as the party trooped off.

Owen, still intent upon his private conversation, followed the Englishman. "Are you a detective, then?" he persisted.

"I suppose I am, in a way," the man replied. "I'm Kevin Keenan."

Owen knew that he was expected to recognize the name, but since he had only been in Britain a week, he hadn't a clue. Except that Kevin Keenan wasn't a famous murderer; he knew all of them. "Oh, really?" he murmured.

"Yes. Just thought I'd have a listen to this tour. It's good stuff. Well presented."

Owen decided that the man must be in show business, perhaps a writer for a BBC crime show. "Are you interested in Ian Brady?" he asked breathlessly. The Moors Murders were among Owen's favorite cases.

Keenan sighed. "Not particularly," he whispered. "But I know that Myra recently came up for parole. She thinks she'll get out, poor cow."

Owen nodded eagerly. He felt as if they were discussing mutual friends. "Do you know anything about the woman in the Crippen case?"

"Ethel LeNeve? Smith was her married name. Oh, she died in 1968," Keenan replied, edging away from Owen.

"It's really great to meet somebody who knows all this!" Owen said reverently. "All my friends think I'm crazy. Can we have a drink after the tour and talk some more?"

The Englishman shrugged. "If they haven't called time by then, I might," he said in weary tones suggesting that he didn't care one way or the other. Kevin Keenan didn't usually enjoy discussing crime with amateurs. They were always asking awkward questions about the Yorkshire Ripper, or wanting to know what it was like behind police lines at death scenes. He had a set of memorized answers that enabled him to hold such conversations without actually listening to them, but occasionally even that proved a bit of a strain.

Owen nodded happily and scurried back to tell Cameron and Elizabeth of his good fortune in finding another expert on crime. They shushed him, too, but he took it in good spirits and settled down to enjoy the remainder of the tour, his brain seething with plans to waylay his new friend immediately afterward and to find out just what his crime-related living actually was. Owen experienced a momentary qualm: suppose the stranger was a criminal? Was there a Mafia in Britain? But this anxiety soon passed. Owen was sure he would never be so lucky as to meet anyone *that* interesting.

Adam Lyal took them down a narrow cobblestone alley, which he said was haunted by the ghost of an old sailor. As he launched into an explanation of the sailor's ill-fated life, a "ghostly" apparition dashed out of the shadows in front of him and lunged at the startled audience, evoking screams from most of the ladies. After a few more menacing gestures aimed at the loudest screamer, the figure ran back into the shadows of a side street. When the tourists had quieted down, the highwayman smiled. "Of course," he said, "I've never seen the ghost myself."

The party continued down the alley to the Grassmarket—the scene of Adam Lyal's demise, he told them. They clustered around the iron-railed plot of grass containing a circular stone monument, the memorial to all those executed in the square over the years.

"Was Burke executed here?" Owen wanted to know.

Elizabeth tugged at his arm. "Hush, Owen! This is a tour, not *Meet the Press*!"

"I'll show you where he used to live—in Tanner's Close," Adam Lyal said patiently.

He led the way up a steep dark street, his cloak flapping about his legs. A wino, cradling his bottle in a paper sack, was settled for the night in a doorway. The noise of so many footsteps shook him out of his stupor, and he looked up just in time to see the chalk-faced ghoul stride past him. After a few moments of startled silence, the derelict called out, "Have ye no been weel, man?"

Cameron and Denny were still snickering at this unscheduled performance when the tour made its next stop, but the highwayman had the last word: "*He* was on the tour last night," he announced.

He launched into a description of the mad old woman said to haunt this particular close, when suddenly the confederate appeared again, this time in a woman's dress and wig, making the tourists scream again and running off into the night as before.

By now the group had discerned the pattern of the tour,

45

so that at each stop, they braced themselves for another fright. Sometimes the accomplice appeared and sometimes he didn't, but the anticipation of his dramatic arrival kept the tension high.

"The ghost is wearing gym shoes!" Denny whispered to Cameron. They had begun to look for the accomplice, to see if they could spot him before he attacked.

"It's a wonderful idea for a tour, isn't it?" Owen said to Elizabeth.

She smiled. "Are you thinking of doing one in America, with all your knowledge of crime?"

Owen shook his head. "American murders are too spread out for a walking tour. And probably too gruesome anyway. Well, I suppose you could do Chicago, but it wouldn't be the same. Mafia executions? Leopold and Loeb killing a little boy? Richard Speck and the eight student nurses? Nobody would pay to see that."

Except possibly you, Elizabeth thought, but aloud she agreed that it wouldn't work as a paying concern.

In the darkest close of all there was not room for the group to form a circle around the guide, so they leaned in clumps against the brick wall of an ancient building, as he paced up and down the cobblestones. "The plague came to Edinburgh, did you know that?" he asked in menacing tones. "It came and went half a dozen times through the Middle Ages, brought from the Continent by . . . rats!"

As he uttered the last word, Adam Lyal's ghostly assistant, his face red-streaked with plague pustules, rounded the corner and drew a squeaking black rat from the folds of his cloak, waving it menacingly at the shrieking tour group. The women in the party shrank back against the building, and

Elizabeth found that she had grabbed Cameron's arm without a conscious thought. After prowling up and down the line of cowering tourists, shaking the rat at those who screamed, the assistant seemed to single out the man in the green anorak. Lunging at him with the rat, as if to cause him to be bitten, the accomplice drew close enough to his victim to speak to him, while those nearby tittered nervously, perhaps in relief that they had not been chosen instead.

After a few moments of terror the assistant dropped the still mewling rat at the feet of a hysterical French girl, and ran out of the close. By that time most of the party had already realized that the creature was only a toy, but the tension of the horror-laden tour and the surrounding darkness had done its work on their nerves, and the screams continued.

The spectral highwayman, amused by his audience's reaction to the trick, leaned against an ashcan, waiting for the panic to subside. When the squeals had died down to a thin murmur, he stepped forward to resume the narrative.

"As I was saying, the plague is no stranger to Britain. In 1348 and again in 1665, the disease arrived on British shores, carried in ships along with—"

He got no further before he was interrupted again, this time by the man in the green anorak, who pitched forward onto the pavement at the highwayman's feet.

In respectful silence, the tourists watched him die.

CHAPTER

6

Owen Gilchrist did not enjoy the murder investigation nearly as much as he might have expected. Someone who doted on true crime stories and biographies of former chief inspectors should have welcomed the opportunity to observe police procedure firsthand, but instead of being thrilled with his good fortune, Owen found himself both uncomfortable at the long wait in the chilly room and oddly apprehensive about his own turn at being questioned.

When the police arrived in Fishers Close to take charge of the corpse and to escort the members of the tour in for questioning, Owen was too nervous to pay much attention to what they did. He found later that he could not remember whether the deceased was covered with a blanket or an oilskin groundsheet, whether the surgeon had arrived with the police or not, and just what was said to him by the officer who noted down his name and address.

He did remember blurting out that he had spoken to the

unfortunate victim. And what had they talked about, please? Well, murder, actually. Despite the chill of the night air, Owen had been sweating when he arrived at the police station. He would probably get pneumonia from it, he thought—another victim for the unknown killer.

Most of the other members of the tour—a women's group from a local church—had been released almost immediately. The archaeologists had been detained, waiting in uncomfortable wooden chairs while the police questioned Adam Lyal himself. Owen wondered why he felt so guilty. Suppose he had to take a lie detector test. What if he failed it simply because he was having an anxiety attack? He wondered if the British police allowed one the customary phone call, and whether the American consul to Scotland would have his home phone number listed in the directory.

Adam Lyal, deceased, had wiped off most of his white stage makeup from the evening's performance, but he still managed to look decidedly pale. The unscheduled demise of a tourist was one surprise that he had not incorporated into the evening's entertainment. As he explained the premise of the tour for the fourth time that evening, he leaned back in the dented metal chair and looked at the linoleum floor instead of at the spotty youth in blue who was meticulously printing ADAM LYAL at the top of his notebook. Gently the guide corrected him, providing the spelling of his real name. The constable looked at him suspiciously: an alias. Adam Lyal was sure that he had just been promoted to the top of a short list of suspects, but he was too tired and worried to be amused.

"Have they found my partner yet?" he asked the young police constable who was taking the statement.

P. C. Hendry took a long look at the smeared vampire makeup and the rumpled black cloak. "There were two of you?"

The tour guide nodded impatiently. "I must have explained this half a dozen times by now! Don't you people talk to each other? When we give the murder tour, I lead the people round and do the commentary; my partner waits for us along the route and makes various surprise entrances in disguise to liven up the tour. Have you found him yet?"

"You are saying then, sir, that it was he who murdered—"

"No, of course, I'm not saying that! Somebody coshed him, and took his place in Fishers Close. You have to find him!"

"I'm sure it's being seen to," the constable said soothingly, scribbling a word on his notepad. "Now, how well did you know the gentleman who was murdered?"

"I hadn't any idea who he was," Lyal replied. "People phone up to reserve a place on the tour, but I don't meet them beforehand. In fact, it is so dark when we begin that I scarcely see them at all."

"Well, we can help you there," P. C. Hendry told him. "There'll be plenty of light in the morgue, and you can go along and look at him for as long as you like. But we have made a tentative identification of the deceased. He was an Englishman called Kevin Keenan. Does that help?"

Lyal shook his head. "Quite a lot of the people who take the tour are from out of town. I take them round in the dark for an hour and never see them again."

"Did the deceased say anything to you during the tour?"

Adam Lyal almost laughed at the constable's formal phrasing. I wonder how many American cop shows he watches per week, he thought. Next he'll be making references to the perpetrator. Suppressing a smile, he turned his attention back to the matter at hand. "Wait . . . somebody asked me a stupid question. What was it? Oh, yes! Whether John Donald Merrett's house was on the tour. But I don't think he asked it. I seem to remember an American accent."

P. C. Hendry hesitated, as if trying to determine what to say next. Sometimes, he decided, you had to give a little information in order to get some. "It sounds like the sort of question Mr. Keenan might have asked," he said. "Considering who he was."

At that moment the door opened, and another officer signaled for their attention. "We've just found the other gentleman who runs the tour," he told Hendry. "He's on his way to hospital with a head injury."

"Thank God for that!" said Adam Lyal. "I've been afraid he was dead."

P. C. Hendry's lips twitched. "No, sir," he said. "Excepting the victim tonight, you are still the only one *deceased*."

In the end Owen had decided against routing the American consul general out of bed, but as he was led away to be questioned, he implored Elizabeth not to leave him alone at the police station. She promised they would wait for him.

"Of course he didn't do it!" Elizabeth said to no one in particular. "He was standing right beside me when the man was stabbed!"

Cameron and Denny ignored her. "Gangs, do you suppose?'' asked Cameron. ''One hears of such things in Glasgow.''

Denny shrugged. ''It's possible, of course, but there was no robbery, and surely that fellow was a bit too old to be mixed up in such things.''

''Will I need my passport?'' Elizabeth asked. ''They always say not to carry it with you, don't they? Or is it not to leave it anywhere?'' She began to rummage through her purse.

''I hope they're not planning to make us stay in town,'' said Denny. ''Imagine telling the old man that the dig has been held up because of a murder.''

Cameron smiled. ''They can hardly detain an entire tour. I believe the parish auxiliary has already been sent home. I think they just want to get the paperwork done. Find out if anyone saw anything, and of course we didn't.''

Elizabeth looked up. ''I did.''

''No,'' said Cameron. ''I mean, if we noticed anything about the killer. All of us saw it happen, more or less, but it was so dark and sudden that we hadn't time to take it in.''

''I did.''

Denny grinned. ''Two days in Edinburgh, and the killer turned out to be somebody you knew, Elizabeth?''

She blushed. ''Of course not! But I did notice his feet. Or rather I noticed the feet of the other one. Adam Lyal's accomplice, I mean. After the first two times, when I was just as startled as everyone else, I noticed that he was wearing white socks and sneakers. His costume always changed, but his footwear didn't. After a while I started looking around for him, because, of course, he was going on ahead and waiting for us to catch up. Once I spotted him waiting for us across the street from one of the closes. But the person who came in during the plague speech—the killer—wasn't wearing white socks and sneakers.''

Cameron sighed. ''So you've just cleared the other tour guide, who has no doubt been found coshed behind an ashcan by now. Very helpful indeed, dear.''

If Owen had not reappeared just then, Elizabeth was sure that there would have been a major Anglo-American disagreement, because her reply would have contained a particularly Anglo-Saxon four-letter word of which Cameron disapproved thoroughly. It was an unladylike utterance, he had informed her more than once. Elizabeth found this attitude very confusing, not only because Cameron himself used the word quite often in reacting to heavy traffic and minor injuries, but also because she had just that afternoon read the Dawson family newspaper and discovered that most of page three consisted of a bosomy young woman, nude from the waist up. When she had asked his brother Ian about this unusual feature for a family newspaper, he seemed surprised that she'd noticed; page three, he explained, was always like that. Elizabeth thought that it was quite hypocritical of Cameron to quibble about a figure of speech and then to drag girlie pictures into the house every day without giving it a second thought. British morals, she decided, were not what she would call consistent.

If he continued to make gentle jokes at her expense for Denny's amusement, they might have words about the British attitude toward women as well, she thought.

Owen, looking more like his Saint Bernard puppy self, interrupted these mutinous thoughts with news of his own.

He appeared to have enjoyed his session with the police hugely.

"I got the constable's autograph!" he announced, in tones suggesting possession of the Hope Diamond, or at least a winning lottery ticket.

"That I would like to have seen," murmured Denny, picturing the spotty young policeman's reaction to celebrity status.

"He was a nice guy," Owen assured them. "Asked me all kinds of stuff about Disney World. Which I haven't been to, but I was able to advise him *not* to make hotel reservations near his cousin's place in Pittsburgh, and then plan to drive down to Orlando for the day." He shook his head. "Boy, you people are really hazy on distances here."

Denny raised his eyebrows. "Did the subject of the recent murder happen to crop up?" he inquired.

Owen nodded, his enthusiasm undampened by the sarcasm. "Sure did! Do you know who that guy was?"

"Elizabeth seems to." Cameron grinned.

Owen ignored the bait. "His name was Kevin Keenan." No signs of recognition lit the faces of his listeners. "Well, *I'd* never heard of him, either," he admitted. "I just thought you guys might have. He was a reporter for the *World Star*. A lady cop came in while I was talking to Donald, and she said they'd called his newspaper back in Britain."

"England!" said Cameron in menacing tones. Why couldn't the bloody Americans get their terms straight? Britain for the whole country; England, Scotland, or Wales for wherever you happened to be.

"Whatever!" Owen shrugged. "Anyhow, she was telling Donald that they said it sounded like Kevin Keenan, from the description on the phone. And you'll never guess what he was doing in Scotland!'' Without waiting for the clever remarks that would surely follow, Owen supplied the answer himself. ''He was working on a story for his newspaper.''

Cameron shrugged. ''The *World Star* is a scandal sheet. I wouldn't use it to wrap fish in.''

''So different from the high journalistic standards of your own dear newspaper,'' Elizabeth purred.

Denny frowned. ''Stop bickering, both of you. Owen, I can't think how you got the police to take you into their confidence, but—''

Owen looked uneasy. ''Well, when the policewoman came in, I said I had to go to the toilet. But I left the door a bit ajar so that I could hear what they said.''

Cameron smirked. ''How very—'' A glance at Elizabeth told him that it would be as much as his life was worth to complete that sentence with the word *American*, as he'd planned. ''—resourceful,'' he finished lamely.

''You'll never guess what he was working on!''

''Tell us,'' Denny suggested.

''He was doing a piece on famous murderers. A where-are-they-now article!''

Cameron blinked. ''What do you mean, where are they now? Peterhead, I should think. And Barlinnie, and Wormwood Scrubbs, and Strangeways—''

''No, not that,'' said Owen. ''Now that you people have abolished capital punishment, most killers get out sooner or later. I guess they go somewhere and start new lives, maybe change their names, if they were well known.''

''And then this reporter comes barging into their lives,

55

telling everyone about their past. No wonder someone murdered him!'' Elizabeth said.

"I wonder who he was looking for in Edinburgh," said Owen. "Merrett has been dead for years. Madeline Smith, the poisoner, died in the twenties. One of the Moors Murderers was from Glasgow; but they're not out, are they?''

"Oh, give it up, Owen!" Denny said. "Keenan's murder was probably not related to his story at all. And even if it were, the murderer would turn out to be some druggie that nobody ever heard of.''

"I suppose so," said Owen, dampened by this dose of common sense.

"And besides," Cameron said, "after tomorrow, you'll be stuck on a barren island in the Hebrides. So there'll be no chance for you to play detective anyhow.''

Owen wasn't listening. "A not-so-reformed killer loose in Edinburgh," he mused. "I wonder how Keenan found him?''

CHAPTER

7

CAMERON

We left Edinburgh early on Sunday morning, when the streets were empty and all the shops were shut, thus relieving Elizabeth of having to decide whether or not she could live without the teddy bear in Waterston's window, the one decked out in the MacPherson tartan.

Perhaps she would have decided against him, anyway; he might have been out of place where she was going, which seemed to be the eighteenth century.

In the car's tape deck she put a cassette of Gaelic folk songs, of which neither of us understands a word, although she claims to know "instinctively" what the songs are generally about. She has learned a few phrases of the language out of one of her interminable books, but her pronunciation is arbitrary, and her fluency nil. Still, whatever ghosts she expects to find in the Highlands would think her very pretty: her hair falls about her shoulders in soft waves, and her dark eyes have a new sparkle of anticipation. She was wearing a

white tapestry skirt and a teal-blue shawl of lambswool, ac-
quired during one of her raids on Princes Street. I said that
I hoped she had more suitable clothing for grubbing about
in the dirt on Banrigh, and she made a face at me and said I
had the soul of a chartered accountant, and that the stone
circle on the island was a Celtic cathedral. I replied that she
could rinse off the sacred soil in holy water if she wanted to,
but she'd better add two cups of Clorox besides. (We were
not amused.)

She paid hardly any attention at all to Glasgow. It is too
rough and modern. Its monoliths are bustling office buildings
of glass and steel, rooted in concrete, rather than the abandoned stone circles of the Hebrides, drifting in mist and
heather. She did not want to stop; nothing there caught her
interest. The Highlands were waiting.

So we left the twentieth century, a rapidly diminishing
vista in the rear-view mirror, and side by side in my brother's
green Moggie Thou, we went our separate ways.

"Oh, ye'll tak' the high road an' I'll tak' the low road."
Elizabeth is too fond of explaining to people that the song
refers to the differing means of travel used by mortals and
fairy folk. The high road would be the motorway of today,
and the low road is the magic passageway used by the *Daoine
Sidhe* to reach their destinations in the twinkling of an eye.
"An' I'll be in Scotland before ye." But will you come to
the same place?

Because we started out with different memories, we were
going to different destinations. The Highlands to me was
scout camporees on the banks of Loch Ness and long
stretches of country roads perfect for trying out my motor-
bike on weekends away from college. But Elizabeth was tak-

ing the low road north. She had visited the Highlands in a stack of books on history and folklore: on her A82 the Campbells massacred the MacDonalds in the glen of weeping, shadowed by *Buchaille Etive Mor*, the rock bastion that supposedly shepherds the pass. Her A830 is a scattering of lochshore caves where the Bonnie Prince hid after the disaster of Culloden.

There are no billboards or convenience stores to pull her back into the twentieth century, and she wrapped herself in the unintelligible Gaelic songs, overlooking the modernity of car and well-paved road.

When she talked to me, it was to tell me tales I'd never heard about the fairy folk, who hid the Sleeping Warriors in the Hollow Hills, in case Britain should ever need them again. And stories of Ossian and Cuchulain, who fought the Norsemen with cold iron and magic. She's had it all out of her books; these tales were not handed down at the fireside by her MacPherson kin, who must all have forgotten about their point of origin several generations before Elizabeth herself existed. Perhaps they had good reason to forget. Such as the New World was two centuries ago, with disease and Indians and only pockets of civilization in a great howling wilderness, the people who went there must have had desperate reasons for going. The Scotland she has returned to is not the one they left; nor is she—the middle-class, college-educated, well-spoken young lady—the same MacPherson who departed these shores so long ago. She could find no more distant strangers, I think, than the ghosts of her own ancestors.

Appalachia has the look of the Highlands, she says, but the New World has more trees. And the people have the same look about them in bone structure, the same fiddle tunes, but even she concedes that the conscious memories of Scotland are generations gone.

"I wonder why we never see the fairy folk in Scotland these days," I said once, in an effort to humor her.

She answered me in Gaelic. I've no idea what she said.

TRAVELER'S DIARY

I'm beginning to understand why my pioneer ancestors stopped their journey in the hills of western North Carolina, rather than pushing on for the plains of the Midwest. They must have thought they were back home. On our drive from Glasgow to Mallaig there were long stretches of landscape that could have been Carolina, if they'd thrown in a few trees. What trees there were turned out to be evergreen; no hardwoods to speak of. I asked Cameron if previous generations had cut down all the good trees for firewood (I can almost sympathize with that; it is July, and I have been so cold at times, I might have burned the Book of Kells to take the chill out of the room), or if hardwood trees have never grown there at all, because of climate, or altitude, or whatever. Of course, he didn't know. To Cameron, Glenfinnan is a brand of Scotch, and Caithness is glass paperweights, not Pictish ruins. How can you get a sense of the past out of someone who cannot even remember the name of his first-grade teacher?

SHARYN MCCRUMB

Even in summer the sky has been a misty gray most of the time, giving a brooding quality to the landscape. You can see for miles on the ribbon of highway through the hills: slippery-looking green mountains dotted with sheep and stone fences, and almost never a sign of human habitation. I would want to live out here in the wilderness, where there'd be nobody else for miles, but the British seem to want to cluster together in cities. I wonder if this is because of land prices, or if it's that the matey ones stayed in Britain, and those who loved solitude (like my kinfolk) left for the New World, where the wilderness went on forever.

Cameron is definitely one of the matey ones. He just loves his apartment back at the university. I told him, "You put me in a box up off the ground, where I can hear folks on three sides through the walls, and I'd be dead in a month." I feel the spell of the mountains and the past very strongly in the north of Scotland, but all of that is lost on Cameron, the seal-man.

On the drive up, I asked him the name of the mountain in the distance. I was looking for Ben Nevis, or perhaps the first of the Five Sisters of Kintail. Cameron glanced at the stark bluish peak across the valley and quipped, "The locals call it Benny Hill." He seemed to find this wonderfully amusing. He was still chuckling over it miles later and didn't seem to notice that I wasn't speaking to him. Then he assumed that I had missed the joke, so he carefully explained to me that *ben* is Gaelic for mountain, and that Benny Hill is a television comedian. I replied that he got full marks for bilingual punning and no credit at all for sensitivity. In fact, he owes points in that category. Cameron's heart is *not* in the Highlands; it is probably not

62

attached to his brain; it may even be in a jar of formaldehyde in an Edinburgh University biology lab.

He looks the part, though. When he isn't being so gratingly *modern*, he could pose for cover art for practically any of those silly romance novels with titles like *Tartan Rapture*. It's the kind of handsomeness that won't change with age. (As a forensic anthropologist, I can tell about things like that.) His looks are in the bone structure, not in what covers them. He'll probably still have those looks at sixty. And despite it all, I hope I will be around to verify that hypothesis. It will probably take till then to break through all that British reserve anyway.

We have until tomorrow morning to reach Mallaig, from which the Calmac ferry departs for the islands beyond, and after that we'll be taken to Banrigh in Cameron's small boat. It will be so fitting, I think, to be crossing the Scottish sea in the same sort of craft my ancestors must have used—a boat like the one Flora McDonald used to take Bonnie Prince Charlie to Skye.

Cameron says that a visit to Culloden Moor would be out of our way, so I will probably have to cry before he will agree to take me. Men can be so difficult at times.

Elizabeth found Mallaig to be a picture postcard sort of fishing village perched between mountain and blue sea. She spent much of the wait for the ferry buying postcards and running around taking photographs, explaining to Cameron, "I must have something to remember this by!" It never seemed to occur to her that she had nothing to remember the village *for*, since she had spent her entire time there storing up memories rather than making them.

The other members of the Banrigh expedition arrived by train, and the group reassembled at a café near the dock, waiting for the Calmac ferry that would take them to the islands beyond.

"Want another meat pie?" Cameron asked Elizabeth. "This is the best meal you'll get for a while."

"I'm not hungry just now," said Elizabeth. "Perhaps I could get one to go."

Cameron and Denny burst out laughing. "It's obvious that you've never had one of these things cold," Denny told her. "Congealed grease! I think I'll have another beer to wash mine down, though I probably shouldn't, as it's pill time."

"Oh, do you have a cold?" Cameron asked.

Denny grinned. "No, just a bit of an infection. My doctor told me to take this antibiotic—ampicillin, I think he said—and to cultivate better taste in women!"

Cameron sighed. "You haven't changed a bit since university."

"And has Cameron changed?" asked Elizabeth.

"Seal-men never change," said Denny. "Except into seals and back."

At a nearby table Owen Gilchrist and Callum Farthing, who had driven over from Inverness, were holding a desultory conversation about American Indian mound builders, because their table-mates, Alasdair and his Danish girlfriend, were talking in urgent whispers and pretending that they were alone at the table.

Gitte, as always, looked nervously obsequious. Like a

whipped hound, Callum thought to himself. He had sized up the med student as a pompous asshole early on and was prepared to have as little to do with him as possible, easier said than done on a tiny island. The girl was a mousy type, rather shaky in her English; he dismissed her at once, thinking that it would be nice to have someone doing the scut work. Cooking detail and washing up—that would be the extent of her usefulness. He wasn't sure about the American one: she looked more capable, but she might be one of those artistic loonies that archaeology seemed to attract. (Callum had once been on a dig with a grandmotherly woman who clanked of turquoise jewelry and wanted to dance naked among the ruins by moonlight.) He smiled to himself: that might be all right; anything to liven up Banrigh.

"Of course, I haven't heard any evidence that the eastern mound builders actually practiced human sacrifice or ritual cannibalism," Owen was saying wistfully.

Callum smiled. The resident loony was present and accounted for.

"Wonderful to be getting away from it all!" Derek Marchand remarked to his assistant.

"Wonderful, indeed," Tom Leath said, through his teeth. He hoped the bottles wouldn't clank in his rucksack. With his luck Marchand would either demand that he pour them out or expect him to share the lot.

"I like the fact that we'll be right away from civilization. It will make me feel more in touch with the people who built this thing. Set up a channel across the centuries, perhaps— no interference." He grinned. "I'm being fanciful—not daft!"

"Right," Leath grunted. "Let's hope they tip you off to some good burial sites. We could do with a major find."

"Like the Viking ship at Sutton Hoo?" Marchand smiled. "That would do wonders for our funding, wouldn't it?"

"We've as much chance of finding Nessie, though."

"Don't be too pessimistic, lad. Our ship may come in."

In fact, it had, but it was the Calmac ferry, a nautical monopoly of the Caledonian MacBrayne Company, which inspired the Scottish doggerel:

> *The earth belongs unto the Lord,*
> *and all it contains,*
> *Except the western highland piers,*
> *and they are all MacBrayne's.*

Elizabeth enjoyed the ferryboat ride very much. Despite a sharp wind from the sea, she spent most of the time on deck, scanning the water for seals and taking photographs of the mainland diminishing in the distance across an expanse of darkest blue. Occasionally, when the wind made her cold, she climbed back into the Dawsons' Moggie Thou, parked with the other cars on the deck, but soon she would brave the elements again, trying for just one more shot of a seabird diving for its dinner. She asked Cameron when they were going to pass the white castle that showed up in all the calendars of Scotland. When he finally realized that she was talking about Eilean Donan, he explained that she could stop waiting for that particular shot: that castle was on the way to the Skye ferry at the Kyle of Lochalsh, and they wouldn't be going anywhere near it.

Elizabeth took it philosophically, saying that castles didn't seem to bring her much luck anyhow.

After several hours of sea watching and picture taking, punctuated by conversations with various members of the expedition over sausage rolls in the snack room, Elizabeth saw the small green point of land appear in front of them. Cameron, who was leaning against the railing, his green windbreaker zipped to protect him from the sea spray, touched her shoulder and pointed to the island. "I guess this is it," Elizabeth murmured, snuggling closer to him.

He nodded. "That white building off to the left is my research station."

"And you'll come to Banrigh every Saturday?"

"Barring bad weather," Cameron said reasonably. "I'm not that good a sailor."

"And will you come oftener if you miss me?"

He smiled. "No. But I'll miss you all the same, hen."

The remainder of the journey to the isle of Banrigh began two hours later, when the diggers and their gear had been transferred from the ferry to the green Moggie Thou—in several trips—and when the gear was stowed away on the old motor launch on loan to Cameron by the foundation for his seal research.

There were more people headed for Banrigh than the launch could comfortably transport, but the trip was a relatively short one—just under an hour, if the wind and weather were good—so it was decided that they would forego the elbow room in the interest of making only one trip.

Elizabeth found the voyage much less enjoyable than she had anticipated. It did not turn out to be a romantic journey, reminiscent of the Young Pretender's sail to Skye, nor was it a quiet time of togetherness before she and Cameron went their separate ways. Elizabeth decided that it was like being in steerage with a party of mental patients. She found herself stuck with Callum, Denny, and Alasdair, all of whom were discussing soccer rivalries, while Cameron had been cornered by Derek Marchand, who wanted to hear about the seal research.

"Not going to kill the beasts, are you?" he asked. "I hear that in Canada they club the young ones for their fur."

"We don't have fur seals," Cameron said politely. "Ours are gray seals, *Halichoerus gryphus*."

"The ones I've seen are brown," said Marchand.

Cameron smiled. "Gray seals can be brown, silver, or any shade of gray."

"And what are you wanting to know. Dietary habits?"

"Oh, no. We know that. They eat herring, halibut, pollack, and even crustaceans. My project is to find out how far they go, and in what direction."

"Going to follow them about, are you?"

"In a high tech way, yes. We've put radio collars on a dozen or so, and I plan to keep track of them electronically."

"Think you can tell a seal from a Russian sub?"

Cameron blinked. "I imagine so, unless one of the crew is wearing a radio collar."

This reply amused Derek Marchand so much that he insisted on repeating the entire conversation to the rest of the party, who smiled faintly and went back to their own conversations.

"So you'll be by every week to bring us supplies and to see your young lady. Very kind of you."

"Not at all," said Cameron, blushing. "Of course, if you need anything urgently, you can always contact me at the station on your radio set. You won't have any range to speak of out here, but your signal ought to reach as far as my research station." His lips twitched. "Or you could try hailing a Russian submarine."

"Perhaps we could catch a passing seal!" Denny said.

"I doubt if you'll see any on Banrigh," Cameron said. "Of course, you might. They've never been tracked before. And nobody lives there to report their presence."

"We'll let you know if we see any," Gitte promised.

Midway through the trip Owen discovered that most of the expedition had not heard about the Witchery adventure and the murder investigation that followed it, and although none of them seemed interested in obtaining such information, Owen insisted on providing it anyway, with heavy emphasis on his cachet as the last person to speak to the deceased.

"And you didn't even find out who he was," Denny reminded him.

Owen shrugged. "Who knew he was going to get himself killed?"

"Some detective you are!" said Elizabeth.

"I don't do well under stress," Owen informed her, "but I'm better prepared now, and I've been thinking a lot about Mr. Keenan's murder."

"I'll let you know if I hear on the news that the Edinburgh police have solved it," Cameron offered.

"And if I solve it first," Owen said, "I'll radio the information to you."

Elizabeth sighed. "Owen, how can you solve the murder

of someone you hardly spoke to, in a country where you don't know a soul, when you are stranded on a barren island miles from civilization?''

"I have my methods!'' Owen smirked. He seemed to be willing to explain them, but at that moment Cameron announced that they were coming in sight of Banrigh, and Elizabeth turned her attention back to the heaving sea and the rocky island still small in the distance.

CHAPTER

8

Banrigh, appearing from a distance like a black seal floating on the surface of the ocean, was one of several thousand uninhabited islands off the northern coast of Scotland. It lay dead and silent in the dark sea, its rocky cliffs shining like bones washed up on the barren beach. In winter the island would be a gray shell shrouded in mist, cold and wet and empty. Even now in the bright summer sunshine some trace of this starkness remained in the sharp outlines of the rocks. The stone circle was not visible from the sea, but its presence seemed to make itself felt, reminding the visitor of prehistoric rituals and sacrifice before the old gods. It made one think, too, of the shipwrecks that must have brought death time and again to the rocky shores.

The passengers in the launch shivered as they looked at the dark island ahead, each thinking that he alone must have imagined such romantic nonsense. But the feeling was there.

Unlike most of Scotland's islands, Banrigh was fertile

enough and just large enough to have supported a struggling population of farmer-fishermen, but by the early twentieth century, the last of the islanders had given up their precarious existence in the back of beyond and had moved to larger islands like Skye. One or two daring ones had even gone as far afield as Inverness on the mainland, leaving the island to the gales and to the ghosts of its ancient inhabitants: those who had built the stone circle, for reasons no one remembered.

Mountains of coarse-grained black gabbro formed the spine of the island, ice-eroded over the centuries into steep-walled corries and long scree runs of broken rock. Over this ancient, sterile skeleton a more recent outcrop of limestone softened the island with stone-studded green fields and a scattering of elder bush and rowan trees. Except for a small plateau on the west side, leading to a rocky channel, three sides of the island were barricaded from the sea by steep bare cliffs that looked axe-carved from a distance, but on the eastern shore the fringe of limestone stretched out to form a rough beach of pebbles and old shells. It was there that the odd private boat would put to shore, mostly Celtophiles or National Trust photographers wanting a look at the Banrigh standing stones. Even that was a rare occurrence. Callanish, the stone circle on Lewis, was both more impressive and more accessible. Banrigh, much off the beaten track, was left alone.

The ruins of the village were visible from the beach; a scattering of "black houses," dirt-floored dwellings built of stacked boulders, with holes in the thatched roofs for the smoke from the peat fire that was kept burning within. The cottages, long unroofed and empty, wouldn't even provide shelter from a mild summer night. Luckily, the Banrigh expedition would not be needing them. The object of their study lay on the other side of the island, as did the island's other ruined dwelling where they were destined to make their camp.

Elizabeth looked about her at the flash of white breakers across the cold blue depths, and at the clouds of lapwing overhead. "This doesn't look anything like Appalachia," she murmured, and Cameron smiled.

Owen Gilchrist hoisted his duffel bag onto a sagging, pudgy shoulder. "How far is it to where we're staying?" he asked plaintively.

"There's a path through the hills there," Tom Leath told him. "What have you got in that thing anyhow?"

"Oh, clothes. A few books. My bagpipes."

Denny snickered. "You've just forfeited any offers of assistance."

"Come along!" said Marchand, slapping Owen's other shoulder. "It's a bracing walk! Lovely weather for it, too!"

"Why didn't you land on the other side of the island?" Owen asked, still trying to think of a way to keep from carrying the heavy duffel bag over a mountain.

"There's just a narrow beach there," Cameron explained, "And the inlet is full of rocks. I didn't trust myself to navigate it, especially with such a crowd on board."

"Are you coming with us?" asked Elizabeth, seeing that Cameron was glancing uncertainly back at his boat. "And don't say that you have to get back to the research station before dark, because God knows when that it is in the summertime. Midnight?"

Cameron grinned. "Very nearly. I should be getting back

and getting things set up for my own project, but I suppose I could give you a hand with some of this gear.''

Alasdair had picked up his own canvas bag and sleeping bag, leaving Gitte's things on the ground at his feet. ''Why couldn't the bloody Navy have built their station on this side of the island?'' he demanded, scowling at the green wall of mountain in front of them.

''Because they were wanting to watch the U-boats on the other side!'' said Denny.

Callum Farthing cleared his throat. ''Actually, I think it was a weather station.''

Tom Leath cast a critical eye at his reluctant troops. ''We'd better get going. It's nearly five now, and we may need all of the available daylight to make the place habitable.''

''The view from the mountain should be very pretty,'' said Elizabeth, looping the camera strap around her neck.

The party began to straggle past the crumbling black houses of the old village, with Denny, the joker as usual, whistling ''The Colonel Bogey March.''

Owen stopped to look at an odd circular thicket near one of the abandoned cottages. ''What a funny hedge! It has a wooden gate attached to the shrubbery, but there's nothing inside. It was too small to fit a house in anyway.''

''It was a garden,'' Gitte told him. ''They planted the hedge to protect it from the winds out here—and from the sheep, of course.''

Owen looked disappointed. ''I thought it might have been a sacred well.''

Gitte stole a glance at Alasdair. He seemed pleased that she had been able to give the American even that simple piece of information. She winked at him, as if to say, "Of course, you knew that, too," although perhaps he had not.

"What a nice path this is!" Elizabeth said when they had gone a quarter of a mile up the gentle slope to the first hill. "Even after all these years the heather hasn't grown onto the path." She stooped to pick a sprig of the tiny purple bloom from the brush. Heather had not been at all the way she had imagined it. Rosebay willow herb, the graceful purple weed that grew as tall as Cameron, was much closer to her expectations, though now that she considered it logically, a short scrubby bush was the logical plant to survive in such a Spartan environment.

Callum Farthing, the young man from Inverness, was walking beside her. "They used this path a lot over the years," he told her, as if to explain why the way was still clear.

"And what are these little piles of stones along the road?" she wanted to know.

"Resting cairns," said Callum. "This was the way to the burying ground, and whenever they rested the coffin along the way, they left a small stone to mark the spot."

Elizabeth stared at the small mound of gray stones. "But not many people lived here."

He shrugged. "Over the years, it adds up."

The path wound its way around the mountain until the village and Cameron's boat were no longer in sight. Elizabeth had been right about the view: from the narrow path she could see gray and green folds of mountains across a narrow valley and the dark blue water shining in the sun beyond that.

Elizabeth, thinking of the ritual signal fires and the stone-circle-as-observatory theory, had expected to find the Banrigh circle at the highest point on the path, but when they had crossed over the summit, she could see the outline of a ring in a field of heather far below. "Why did they put it in the valley?" she wondered aloud.

Cameron smiled. "Would you want to drag stones that large up this mountain?"

"Perhaps not," Elizabeth said after some consideration. "But if I were going to put that much work into a project, I'd sure want everybody to see it."

Derek Marchand spotted the stone circle a few moments later, and he halted the procession on the path and pointed it out to everyone. "There it is! The object of our quest."

"Should be a good spot for overhead shots of the site," Tom Leath muttered to Callum Farthing.

"We will visit the circle tomorrow," Marchand was saying. "I'm greatly tempted to march you all there tonight, but I feel sure that we will need every moment of daylight to work on our own living quarters.

"Thank God he's got some sense of priorities!" Alasdair muttered.

"Also from here you can see the very small island just a few hundred yards from Banrigh, with one large stone on it. We shall be sending someone there to do more measurements as well."

"I can't swim!" Denny quipped.

"There's supposed to be an old rowboat near the military hut," Leath informed him.

Elizabeth focused her camera on the stone circle glinting in the sunlight far below, trying to get the smaller island in the background of the shot. "I hope this turns out," she murmured.

"So do I," said Cameron. "In more ways than one."

"Good view from up here," Alasdair said approvingly. "I'll bet the old boys could see the Viking raiding parties from miles away. Not much they could do about it, though, I guess, except stash the valuables under a rock."

Gitte Dankert did not smile. She was not amused by jokes about her bloodthirsty Norse ancestors; in fact, she found it most embarrassing that she should somehow be allied to the destruction blamed on her ancestors. She hoped she wouldn't have to endure teasing on the subject from her fellow diggers; after all, many of the island dwellers of Scotland were closely related to the Scandanavians both by blood and by culture, and she knew that she would be most helpful in pointing out similarities.

Alasdair was still examining the island from this bird's-eye view. His eyes flickered from the glint of the stone circle in the sunlight to the bright green grass of the peat fields dotted with white-flecked boulders. A narrow burn sparkled amid the heather. "I don't see any obvious burial sites," he grunted.

"I do," said Callum Farthing. "Several. But I'm afraid they're not of the period we're investigating."

"Burial sites? Where?" Owen's gothic soul was stirred out of fatigue and into something like animation. "How can you tell?"

Callum smiled. "Later. We have work to do."

* * *

The Nissen hut, erected by the Royal Navy during World War II, looked like an overturned tin can half buried in the dirt. It was a windowless cylinder, thirty feet long, and just high enough to stand up in. Despite forty years of salt air and neglect, it was still in good shape, with only a few rust spots in its metal exterior and no sign of roof leaks on the dirt floor within. The interior had been partitioned off, probably to separate sleeping quarters from work areas, but now the shell was empty, except for a long wooden table and a few scraps of yellowed paper still posted here and there. The bare light sockets dangled from the ceiling; both bulbs and electricity had vanished long ago.

"This is rather primitive," said Alasdair, looking around. "We might be better off in tents."

Derek Marchand smiled. "Yes, I had decided that myself. I spent enough time in these during the war, so I brought my one-man tent. A bit of damp is a small price to pay for a bed under the stars."

"We can set the radio up on that half of the table," Tom Leath said. "There ought to be room enough for us to eat on what's left. I'm sleeping outside, too," he added.

"I thought the ladies might like to have one of the partitioned spaces," said Marchand.

Elizabeth smiled weakly at Gitte Dankert. She supposed she would have to think of something to make conversation about9 but the prospect was not inviting. What, she wondered, do you discuss with a Danish geisha?

"Would anyone like some tea?" she asked brightly.

In order to prepare tea, Callum Farthing had to assemble the Camping Gaz, the two-burner butane stove that would serve them for cooking and heating. By the time he had the stove working and Gitte had brought a pail of water from the burn, it was nearly seven o'clock, but the blue had not begun to fade from the sky.

"One cup of tea," said Cameron, "and then I really have to be getting back."

Elizabeth nodded. "I wish . . ." What? she thought. That he didn't have to go, or that I could go and help him? That the islands were closer together than they are? "I wish I were a seal."

"I'll be back on Saturday. Let me go and say goodbye to Marchand."

"Shall I walk you back to the boat?" Elizabeth asked.

Cameron shook his head. "You have enough to do here. This place could do with a good scrubbing."

Elizabeth spent the remaining daylight hours helping Gitte scour the Nissen hut, not because she wanted to, and not because she thought it needed to be as clean as Gitte was determined to get it. In the middle of the room Callum Farthing was setting up the radio, seemingly oblivious to both their conversation and their labors.

"It has a dirt floor!" Elizabeth said once in exasperation. "How clean can you get it? Besides, we're not going to do brain surgery here!"

Gitte didn't answer directly. She very seldom did. She went on scrubbing the side of the partition. After a few minutes she said, "I'm sure I can manage by myself."

Elizabeth sighed and picked up the bucket. If there was anything she hated more than boredom, it was guilt. "I'm going for some more water from the bur-rrn,'' she announced.

Gitte kept scrubbing. ''You don't sound Scottish.''

Elizabeth consoled herself with the thought that she didn't have to hurry back with the pail of water. Fetching it at all was a splendid gesture of cooperation; there was no need to be fanatic. Besides, she could explore the island tomorrow. It had better not rain tomorrow! she thought.

Across the fields she could see Leath and Marchand at the stone circle. She wondered where the others were. Probably making landmark discoveries in Scottish archaeology, she thought. Probably finding solid gold Viking ships and a Celtic Rosetta Stone, describing in clearly carved runes just exactly how to use a stone circle. ''And I will have helped to clean a Nissen hut,'' she said aloud.

She missed Cameron already. She stood for several minutes on the cliff above the rocky cove, trying to catch a glimpse of the small white boat among the whitecaps, but it never appeared.

Suddenly, a moving square of red on the shore caught her attention. It was Denny, walking along the water's edge, examining shells.

''Hey!'' she yelled. ''How did you get down there?''

Denny looked up and waved. He pointed to an outcrop of rocks a few hundred yards along the cliff. Elizabeth hesitated. She ought to be heading in the other direction, but then it occurred to her that brine would be an even better disinfectant than fresh water, so she waved back at Denny and hurried along the path at the edge of the cliff.

A natural way down the cliffs, probably improved by the original inhabitants of the Nissen hut, was still discernible, although crumbling rocks and sudden zigzags indicated that it had not been used for many years. Elizabeth, who did not quite trust her running shoes for mountain climbing, took a long time to pick her way down through the rocks, holding on to a jutting boulder as often as she could on the descent. Finally, she reached the bed of smooth pebbles that constituted the so-called beach of Banrigh's western side.

"Where have you been keeping yourself?" Denny asked. "I thought Cameron had taken you away with him."

"No such luck," said Elizabeth. "I've been helping Gitte clean our living quarters."

"And you'll be fixing dinner, then, soon, I suppose?" asked Denny with a look of careful innocence.

Elizabeth paused long enough to count to ten before answering. "I suppose I could," she replied. "And after dinner we can draw up the chart to see whose turn it will be tomorrow."

Denny laughed. "So you're not just a girlfriend along for the ride?"

"No," Elizabeth said, "I'm not. I don't know much about British archaeology, but I've had enough experience back home, and I intend to learn a lot while I'm over here." She looked around at the wall of rocks behind them and at the ripples of water splashing gently on the pebbles. "Which reminds me. What are you doing down here?"

Denny shrugged. "Just messing about, I suppose. Getting the lay of the land. I've proved Cameron wrong already. There was a seal here when I came down. Cute little bugger, sunning himself on a rock near the shore. I didn't scare him off, either. I think he left to go fishing."

"I hope he comes back," Elizabeth said. "I haven't seen a seal before. Except in zoos, I mean. Never out in the wild."

"Really?" said Denny. "I thought they were quite common out in California."

"Everything is quite common out in California!" Elizabeth quipped. "I happen to be from Virginia."

"Well, if the seal turns up again, I'll give you a shout," Denny promised.

"Yes, we ought to tell Cameron about him."

"Something tells me he'll find out on his own," Denny said. "The beastie was wearing a wee black collar around his neck."

Owen had found Alasdair walking alone on the cliffs and had tagged along, despite the pointed lack of an invitation to do so. "This is a very dramatic place!" he remarked. "It could be any century at all, couldn't it?"

"I suppose so," Alasdair said politely.

"And with such a bloody history!"

"I beg your pardon?"

"Violent, I mean," Owen corrected himself, suddenly remembering what his original adjective meant in Britain. "Viking sea raids! Druid sacrifices! Imagine the ghosts that must walk these hills!"

Alasdair summoned up a frosty smile. "I hardly think it was quite the pageant that you imagine. I rather think it was countless years of tedium, of dull little nobodies scratching out an existence on a seabound rock, stinking of peat smoke and sheep shite."

Owen blinked at this outburst, He was not sure what *shite* was, but he rather thought it must be what it sounded like.

"But surely you're interested in their way of life," he stammered.

"Not particularly," said Alasdair, walking faster. "I think the common man has always been pretty much the same, from Babylon to Bearsden. What interests me are those who take charge of the common man. The leader for whom the great tomb is built, for whom the gold is fashioned into ornaments."

Owen nodded. "That's just how I feel about murderers! I mean, money isn't the only measure of a powerful person. Murderers are usually highly intelligent, and they're trying to get out of adversity by following their own rules. They're crazy, of course," he added, seeing the look on Alasdair's face.

"You haven't much of a sample to judge from, have you?" Alasdair smiled. "Since you can only judge by the ones who were caught. And who knows what percentage that is? By definition, the very best of the breed are never considered at all."

Owen shrugged. "Well, maybe a few were just caught by bad luck, but in general I guess you're right. I'd say the guy who killed Keenan in Edinburgh was a leader type. Imagine killing someone in front of a whole alleyful of witnesses!"

"Well, it was dark, wasn't it?" Alasdair pointed out. "Not much risk there, considering the slow reflexes of the average person in shock. Still, that's only rebellion on a small scale, in our tight little society of today. They're hardly worth your obsession. The true rebels lived centuries ago, when you could level whole kingdoms, not just individuals. When murder was a privilege of the elite, and no one questioned it. I hope that we will find evidence of such a great one here.''

"I don't think there were any big shots here on Banrigh," said Owen, scratching his head. "Skye, maybe."

Alasdair pointed to the standing stones, shining red in the slant of the evening sun. "Somebody who *was* somebody was here."

CHAPTER

9

By ten o'clock the sky was a sheet of copper, streaked with thin black clouds against the silhouettes of the mountains. The diggers had taken their dinner plates outside, where they sat on the rocks watching the sunset.

"Nature's fireworks!" Marchand said, waving his fork at the sky.

Owen shoveled a heaping forkload of rice into his mouth. "What is this stuff?"

"Chicken curry," said Denny. "Invented by the Indians, but cooked by the Danes, I believe."

Gitte smiled. "I enjoy to cook," she said.

Elizabeth, who had done at least half of the preparation of the meal, noticed the conspicuous lack of credit given to the American contribution, but she decided that it was not worth mentioning, since dinner had turned out to be considerably less of a production than she had expected. The provisions for the expedition consisted almost entirely of packets of dehydrated stews and curries, to which one added water, and which were then heated in a saucepan on the camp stove. Elizabeth decided that it didn't really matter who did the cooking, since it was hardly any bother at all. Even so, she would have preferred not sharing the task with Gitte. The cooking was nothing; listening to Gitte run on about Alasdair's preferences in food and the restaurant they went to on his birthday—that was a chore! She considered asking Denny to help her with future meals, but as soon as she thought of it, she realized that she would never get this plan past Gitte. No meal would be prepared except under Gitte's supervision—with all credit going to her. If Marchand was the father of the expedition, Gitte seemed determined to be the mother.

"Can we get any news on the radio?" Elizabeth asked Callum.

Callum Farthing laughed. "It isn't that kind of radio," he told her. "It's just for sending messages over a distance of a few miles. Something like your CB in the States."

"Besides," Gitte said, "it is very late, and we should all go to sleep now so that we can begin working early tomorrow." She began to gather up the plates.

Elizabeth sighed. "Is it very far from here to Cameron's island?" she asked Denny.

He shrugged. "In comparison to what? You saw how long it took this afternoon. Why do you ask?"

"I was thinking of swimming it."

Although the sky was cloudy, it was already well past dawn by seven o'clock. By then the camp was stirring. Gitte had taken the water bucket with her when she went to the burn for her morning ablutions. Shortly after her return she had managed to wake everyone up—with a combination of coffee smells and a rendering of "Blowin' in the Wind," in Danish and off-key. Breakfast was powdered eggs and stewed tomatoes, and Elizabeth was glad to let Gitte have the credit for its concoction.

"Do we have any marmalade for this bread?" asked Denny, eyeing the untoasted lump on his plate.

"There's something in a jar on the table," Elizabeth replied. "Shall I get it?"

"Hold it!" Owen called after her. "Was it an old mayonnaise jar with no label? I thought so. That's not to eat. It's a honey-and-wax mixture. For my bagpipes," he added, seeing the others' puzzled expressions.

"You feed your bagpipes?" Elizabeth asked.

"That's exactly what it's called!" Owen said eagerly. "Feeding the bagpipes! The inner bag is leather, and you have to keep it lubricated so that it won't crack and split."

"Can't you just use saddle soap?"

"No. There are commercial preparations that you can use nowadays, but the traditional treatment has always been honey and hot wax. I thought, being an archaeologist and all, I'd like to stick with tradition."

Denny nodded. "*Stick* with tradition, indeed. So you're going to pour this gunk down your bagpipes?"

"Tonight after dinner."

"And then I suppose you won't be able to play them for . . . oh . . . at least a week?" Elizabeth said hopefully.

"They should be okay by tomorrow."

"Here is your marmalade, Denny," said Gitte, holding

out a small white jar. "I brought some myself." She smiled triumphantly at Elizabeth.

Elizabeth smiled back with equal warmth. "How very clever of you," she said.

As they finished their coffee, Tom Leath outlined the plans for the day. "We're going to do background work," he explained. "This site has never really been studied, so the more we find out about this island, the better off we'll be. I want soil samples taken—that's you, Alasdair—not only from the stone circle, but also from the peat, the field of heather, and so on. Check for chalk dust, outcroppings of rock—anything we ought to know about."

"Right," Alasdair said. "I know the drill. And I'll work alone."

Leath ignored this remark and the hurt look that crossed Gitte's face. "And, Denny, you need to take the surveying equipment up the mountain and give us some general plans of the site."

"Can I poke about a bit while I'm up there?" Denny wanted to know.

"Not today," Marchand said. "We need the overview before we go on with the main focus of our project."

"Okay." Denny nodded. "It'll keep."

"What will keep?" Elizabeth whispered.

"Callum, you'll be doing the photography, of course," Leath told him. "We need some shots from above, from where Denny is surveying, but also close shots of the circle itself from various angles. Marchand and I will be walking around the island looking for other signs of the culture of the circle builders. Grave sites, a *broch* . . . whatever."

"What about me?" Elizabeth asked.

"You'll be digging an exploratory trench just beyond the circle itself. Go down a few inches by shovel, and then trowel. We want soil layers, evidence of chalk. Bones if we're lucky."

"Gold bracelets if we're *really* lucky," Denny called.

"Gitte can help you," Leath continued.

"Oh, no!" Elizabeth said too quickly. "I don't need any help at all!"

After a short, embarrassed silence Denny spoke up again. "I could use a hand with the surveying, then. Somebody needs to note down the figures and all that. I'd be glad of your help, Gitte."

She smiled and nodded. "Yes, Denny, of course."

Elizabeth felt guilty again. I suppose I ought to beg her pardon, she thought, but then I'd feel guilty for lying.

"What about me?" Owen asked plaintively.

"Not forgotten," said Leath, consulting his notes. "You're to have a look at that monolith on the wee island offshore. Just find out all you can. Whether the rock matches the stone circle; type of soil; angle in relation to the circle . . . Any questions?"

Owen frowned. "I didn't see a boat. Did you see a boat?"

"There's supposed to be an old rowboat beside the hut here."

"Where?" Owen asked.

"Right," said Leath. "Gilchrist, your assignment is to find the bloody rowboat. Any other questions?"

"Just one." It was Denny. "What time is lunch?"

* * *

The morning passed quickly for Elizabeth. She had someone to talk to for most of the morning. First, Alasdair appeared with his auger and plastic bags to collect the first in his series of soil samples.

"Yours is an interesting job," she told him. "You might find all sorts of things buried here."

Alasdair smiled. "Perhaps you're thinking of metal detectors," he said. "I'm just differentiating between loam and sand—that sort of thing."

Elizabeth reddened. "Yes, I know about soil sampling," she told him. "I'm getting a master's in forensic anthropology, and we find soil analysis useful. I was thinking that you might find evidence of, say, human sacrifice in the soil. Like the bog people in Scandinavia."

Alasdair smiled. "I doubt there were any ritual burials in this peat bog. I suppose it would preserve the bodies well enough because of the high acidity and natural formalin, but I'm not likely to stumble across anything spectacular on a random soil sampling. I doubt that we shall find anything at all dramatic here. I fear we'll dash the hopes of your fellow countryman."

Elizabeth sighed. "Owen is a bit gung ho, isn't he? He's very new at archaeology, and I'm afraid he's based his impressions on *Raiders of the Lost Ark*."

"This should set him to rights, then," said Alasdair, emptying the core of soil into his plastic bag. "I'm sure I shall find nothing more exciting than a few dead sheep."

By the time Callum had finished the overhead photographs of the stone circle, taken from the path on the mountain, Elizabeth had begun to trowel away the soil in her trench, a few millimeters at a time.

"Am I in your way?" she asked as he adjusted the focus of his camera.

"Not yet. Want a picture of yourself with the circle behind you?"

Elizabeth touched her hair, which had been thoroughly tangled by a morning of sea winds. "What do I look like?"

Callum looked up from the viewfinder. "Very American," he told her.

Elizabeth frowned. "You're the one with a camera around your neck."

"The sweatshirt's a dead giveaway. Very collegiate."

"Oh, the outfit," Elizabeth said. "That's what everybody wears on digs. I always thought I looked sort of Celtic, though, with my dark hair and blue eyes."

Callum shrugged. "I suppose so. I always think of them as redheads, myself."

Since Callum himself had bright red hair, Elizabeth decided that this was a form of projection and that it didn't bear arguing about. She put down her trowel and posed in front of the largest stone of the circle. She turned her profile to the camera and stared out to the sea with what she hoped was a brooding expression. She tried to capture the mood of an ancient Celt by imagining one of the Highland legends: crashing breakers turning into demon horses to carry away drowned sailors; a young girl waiting for a ship that never comes; an island woman watching the empty sea for her selkie lover . . .

"Now how do I look?" she asked Callum, trying not to move her lips.

He shrugged. "Dunno. Bit like one of those perfume commercials, I s'pose. The ones that try for a mood instead of bludgeoning you with the product. What would you be selling? Old Spices for Ladies, if there is such a thing. Or some wild West scent. Old Cowhide?''

"You Scots are a romantic lot!" Elizabeth grumbled.

"We are," said Callum, "but we're not much on pretense. It isn't something that you play at. It happens—or it doesn't.''

She nodded. "Mostly it doesn't.''

Alasdair set down the bag of soil and glanced at his watch. It was nearly the hour the others had agreed on for lunch, but he was not hungry, at least not hungry enough to give up his solitude for the trivial banter of his fellow workers. He rather enjoyed being alone with his thoughts and with the rough beauty of the island. Perhaps he could buy it someday, when he had made a success of his medical career. People did own islands, he knew. They even built very grand houses on them. He stretched his long legs out in the grass, thinking for just a moment of sheep droppings. But no, it had been a good many decades since sheep had grazed the fields on Banrigh. He liked the feel of the sun on his face—really lovely weather they were having, and not something you could take for granted in the islands. It was bound to rain sooner or later. Another good reason not to go back for lunch. He'd better get as much done as he possibly could, in case the weather didn't hold.

Alasdair did not mind hard work, not even menial work, as long as he felt that he was appreciated, that his work was contributing to his future. The archaeological expedition might seem an odd choice of holiday for a medical student, but he liked the idea of being *the* physician for the crew, and he thought that archaeology was a rather posh hobby for one to have. The right sort of people had an interest in antiquities; it might serve him well in the future.

He smiled to himself. Besides, there was always the promise of adventure, which appealed to him. The crass little American might be right about treasure in the Highlands. There were certainly enough legends about it. Alasdair would be glad of a bit of treasure; he could use it more than the Crown could. It was a bit tiresome, at times, being all alone in the world and having to associate with scores of rich kids whose parents were seeing them through medical school with cars, flats, and a decent allowance, while Alasdair the Orphan worked and scrimped and studied hard to keep up with them. He was going to make it, though. Nothing was going to hold him back.

Idly, he began to scratch in the soil with the auger. Hello! What was that? . . . Nothing he need mention, he decided a few moments later. Lunch was definitely out.

"How did your morning go?" Elizabeth asked Denny in a carefully neutral tone.

"Just as you think it did, I'm sure," he murmured, scooping up the last bit of canned spaghetti from his tin plate. "She's bloody hopeless, is Gitte. Tell her everything twice, and she still gets it wrong! We managed, though. I finally let her hold the clipboard when I wasn't using it, and that was the extent of her assistance."

"I wonder if I'd be the same way if I were trying to help Cameron in his work."

"I shouldn't think so," said Denny. "You're the competent sort, aren't you?"

Elizabeth sighed. "I wonder if I am. Look at this." She held up a forefinger with a small jagged cut just beginning to scab.

"How did you do that?" Denny asked. "That's bad-looking."

"I was walking along the shore just before lunch, and I saw something metal in the sand, so I ran and pulled on it." She grinned. "I guess I had caught some of Owen's madness! I was expecting to find the Lord of the Isles' crown, at the very least."

"And it was . . . ?"

"A rusty old piece of metal. Probably off a shipwreck, or even an old tin can! And I got cut trying to retrieve it. That will teach me to go chasing treasure!"

"It's more than a scratch," Denny said, inspecting her hand. "What have you done about it?"

"Well, I dipped it in the ocean. And I did think of showing it to Alasdair, but he didn't turn up for lunch. Besides, I'm not sure I'd like the idea of being his patient —not after listening to Gitte run on about him by the hour. Anyway, it's not that bad."

"Well, I can see how you wouldn't want Alasdair putting on his doctorly airs for you, but I don't think you can risk getting it infected. Not with us grubbing about in the dirt and all. You'll fetch up with lockjaw if you're not careful. Here, I tell you what—" He fished in the pocket of his trousers and brought out a small plastic bottle. "I'll share my antibiotic tablets with you. They're strong stuff; ought to keep the finger germs at bay."

"Oh, I couldn't take your medicine."

"Go on!" he urged. "This is my second bottle. I'm nearly well, I swear it. This is just my doctor making sure. Go on—take one!"

He shook one small white tablet out of the bottle and put it in her hand. "Okay," Elizabeth said. "I guess it couldn't hurt to take one."

"One a day," said Denny. "We'll give it a week, and if your finger doesn't fall off, we'll pronounce you cured."

Elizabeth laughed. "If I remember to take them."

Owen Gilchrist wondered if the British had ever heard of snipe hunts. More specifically, he wondered if sending him in search of a rowboat had been a British variant of the wild goose chase, because he had not found any sign of a rowboat. He had spent the entire morning wandering around the island like Banquo's ghost, and he hadn't accomplished anything, except to get his month's quota of exercise and more fresh air than he ever wanted.

The dig was beginning to strike Owen as rather a closed shop. Callum was the photographer; Alasdair tested soils; Denny did the surveying. Owen felt that he and the two women were afterthoughts, but he wasn't sure what he could do about it. He was not familiar with British archaeology, and he did not have enough experience to handle any job without supervision, but surely they should be teaching him something. He ought to be good for more than chasing nonexistent boats.

He was afraid that, as usual, he was getting a reputation as an eccentric clown. The bagpipes—they all enjoyed ragging him about that. And perhaps he'd been too enthusiastic about his fascination with crime. But he wasn't stupid, or even incompetent. Owen decided that his fellow workers' attitude was their problem. He certainly didn't intend to alter his personality just to conform with their dull conventionality. Of course, he reflected sadly, he wouldn't have any friends—but he was used to that.

That evening, while they were waiting for their dinner to complete the interminable process of heating up on the Camping Gaz stove, Derek Marchand insisted that each of them give an account of his day.

Alasdair explained in considerable detail exactly what sorts of soil samples he had taken and added that he could use another day or so to complete his testing.

"What did you find?" Owen asked.

Alasdair favored him with a cold smile. "The soil is acidic, of course. Peat bogs on top of limestone. I'm afraid I can't get much more specific than that. We send the samples back to the mainland to be analyzed."

Owen reddened. "Yes, I knew that! I just wondered if you'd found anything of interest."

Another smile. "A cache of Celtic gold, for example?"

Tom Leath pointed out that there had been gold found from that era on other Scottish islands.

"In the Orkneys," Alasdair reminded him.

"I read about a legend once concerning a French ship that left thirty thousand pounds in gold for Bonnie Prince Charlie," Denny said. "No one has ever found that, have they?"

"Not officially," Callum Farthing said. "But I can

promise you that it didn't last much past 1745. The MacDonalds probably spent the lot.''

"Be that as it may," Derek Marchand said, "we are not here to hunt treasure, but to find knowledge. I personally would rather confirm the existence of a megalithic yard than uncover a trunkful of gold trinkets from some ancient lady's boudoir.''

"How very noble of you," Alasdair drawled.

"Right," said Tom Leath, taking his cue from the expedition leader. "Let's get back on track, then, shall we? We were in the midst of discussing our day's activities.''

Callum produced a list of the photographs that he had taken. He and Marchand discussed what other ones might be necessary.

Denny discussed the results of the day's surveying without any mention of Gitte's incompetence.

"I didn't find the boat," Owen said when his turn came. He explained that he had searched most of the shoreline, the huts in the village at the other side of the island, and even among the trees, looking for a hidden rowboat, but there was none to be found.

"That's odd!" said Marchand. "I was told there was one kept here.''

"Did you try the cave?" Callum Farthing asked.

Owen frowned. "Cave?"

"Yes. If you walk along the beach below the cliffs, and then climb over the rocks, you'll find a small cave cut into the cliffs. I imagine the sea goes well into it at high tide, but when I went in this afternoon, it was dry enough.''

"Sounds like Sawney Bean's place," Owen grunted. "What makes you think the boat would be in there?''

"It seems a logical place to put it to protect it from the elements. Anyhow, that's where it is. I saw it there this afternoon, up on a sort of ledge about twenty yards back from the mouth of the cave."

"I didn't check along the beach," Owen muttered defensively.

"Well, perhaps it did take a bit of finding," Marchand said soothingly. "But now that we've located it, you can start checking that heelstone on the little island. I think that can wait until day after tomorrow, though. I want everyone to pitch in at the main site tomorrow."

"Okay," Owen said. "I think I'll go off and read now."

After a few more minutes' conversation around the camp fire, Elizabeth decided to go and check on Owen. It wasn't that she felt any kinship with him because they were both Americans, but she did feel sorry for him, because he seemed to be the underdog of the camp. Besides, she told herself, if I can only dislike one member of the expedition, it's going to be Gitte, so I have to be nice to poor Owen. She found him sitting at the long table in the Nissen hut, studying his crime books.

"I thought you were going to feed your bagpipes tonight," she said, pulling up the other chair.

"I can do that tomorrow," Owen grunted. "I might want to play some later tonight. Anyhow, I wanted to read up on these cases."

"*Who's Who of British Murderers*. Very wholesome, Owen."

He scowled. "I'm not reading this for *fun*. Not this time anyhow. Remember what the policeman told me?"

"As I recall, nobody told you anything. I believe you were eavesdropping—"

Owen waved away this detail. "Whatever. I *found out*, if you insist on being technical, that Keenan was researching a piece on paroled killers. Where are they now? Obviously one of them was in Edinburgh."

"I agree with that," Elizabeth said, "since Keenan was apparently there to interview somebody, but I don't think you can assume that whoever it was murdered him."

Owen sighed. "If the police are as naïve as you are, I'd better hurry and figure this case out, because otherwise there'll be no hope of finding the murderer."

Elizabeth decided that arguing with somebody, even if he was wrong, did not constitute cheering him up. "All right, Owen," she said. "I'll keep an open mind. What have you got so far?"

Owen brightened. "I ruled out all the famous criminals because I'd know if they had been paroled, and they haven't been. I also ruled out the mundane ones, for obvious reasons."

"It isn't obvious to me. What, exactly, is a mundane murder?"

"Someone who kills while burglarizing a house, or hits somebody too hard in a bar fight or kills his wife in a drunken rage. Those people wouldn't make very interesting reading in a tabloid story. Usually they are just poor and trapped."

"There is a certain logic there," Elizabeth conceded. "You assume that Mr. Keenan would have been looking for sensational cases to sell newspapers. Somebody famous enough for people to remember the crime, but not so famous that people have kept up with him. Did you find any murderers who fit the bill?''

"Quite a few. But the snag is that I don't know where they are now. Boy, I would love to have read Keenan's article. What a great story! Too bad he didn't get to write it."

Elizabeth shivered. "I should think you'd have had enough horrors watching someone actually die."

"It didn't seem very real, did it? Anyway, it all happened so fast, and it isn't as if we knew him. Don't you think he'd be pleased that I'm trying to track down his killer?''

"He was a reporter. I suppose he might."

"I think so, too. Here are the ones I've considered so far." He pulled a small sheet of paper out of the back of the book and showed her a list of names. "I kind of like this one. Fifteen years ago a little boy was strangled in Newcastle, and the killer turned out to be one of his playmates—an eight-year-old girl! She was sent to a mental institution, but supposedly she was released at age twenty-one."

Elizabeth shivered. "Cured, I hope?"

Owen shrugged. "You never know. She sounds like a psychopath to me. Someone who doesn't feel the difference between right and wrong, but who just has to learn to obey the laws through fear of society's retribution."

"Thank you. I know what a psychopath is," Elizabeth snapped. "I have a bachelor's degree in sociology."

Owen smirked. "Guess you know what poverty is, too, then."

"I'm going to grad school."

"Wise move. Okay, next case. This guy would be pretty old now. He was a soldier in World War II, and he was engaged to this girl, and then he found out she was a local prostitute, so he killed her and hid her body in a tank on the army base. Pretty weird, huh? At the trial they claimed he'd been visiting the body for a couple of days and fixing its makeup and changing its clothes."

"Ugh!" said Elizabeth. "I suppose he went off to Valium Village as well?"

"Oh, yeah. Broadmoor, I think. But when these old geezers pass sixty, they usually get released quietly. Unless the crime was too notorious. That sort of killer is pretty safe after sixty. Diminished sex drive, you know. Remember Ed Gein, the cannibal murderer in Wisconsin?"

"No."

"Oh! Well, he's the guy that the movie *Psycho* was based on, but the real case was much more interesting. Ed died in a mental institution, because people stayed grossed out about his crimes for *decades*, but I'm sure he wouldn't have done anything if they'd let him out."

"I can understand their being unwilling to risk it, Owen."

"Oh, sure. The publicity is deadly. Once they make a TV movie of your case, you're in for good. John Wayne Gacy . . . Ted Bundy . . . Charlie Manson . . . no way they're getting out."

"Do they have TV movies in Britain?" Elizabeth asked.

Owen shrugged. "Not that I know of, but they have the same kind of publicity. The Yorkshire Ripper isn't coming out, I can tell you that. But this guy here, I bet he's out, or soon will be. Alec Evans.''

Elizabeth took the book and read aloud the entry that Owen had marked in red. '' 'Glasgow. Poisoned his entire family with thallium in the sugar bowl. Considered a brilliant young man, very good in chemistry.' ''

Owen snickered. "Well might they say so. Thallium was a very good choice. It's slow, and it hits everyone in different ways so that the causes of death appear different: meningitis, pneumonia, and so on.''

"He poisoned his whole family!'' said Elizabeth, still reading. ''And he was only fourteen years old.''

"Kids don't have a lot of self-control anyway,'' Owen said. "I guess he got angry with them and booby-trapped the sugar bowl. Probably too immature to know the finality of it.''

"I think fourteen is old enough to grasp the concept of death.''

"Well, so do I,'' Owen agreed. ''And I'll bet he's another psychopath, but I'll also bet you that he gets out. Because he was so young when he did it.''

"How do you sleep at night, Owen?''

He grinned. "Oh, these guys are pretty rare. Most of them don't kill men anyhow. Now the last one here is the best bet, I think.''

Elizabeth consulted the book. "Hmm. From Edinburgh. Malcolm Allen. At age sixteen, he raped and killed a nine-year-old girl in a public park. In *Scotland*?''

Owen grinned. "It's a bad old world these days, even in sleepy Scotland.''

"I guess it always was, what with Sawney the Cannibal

wandering around a few centuries ago. You just don't think of things like that when you see the travel posters. All the castles and kilts and all that.''

"Your boyfriend is from Edinburgh, isn't he? I wonder if he knows anything about these cases? Especially the Malcolm guy.''

"Don't bet on it." Elizabeth smiled. "Unless one of the killers is a seal, he will have escaped Cameron's notice.''

"I wish we could have stayed in Edinburgh longer. I'd like to check newspaper morgues about these cases. See if there were any articles on release dates for these four.''

"You can always do it when we go back," said Elizabeth. "That is, if the police haven't solved Keenan's murder by then.''

Owen brightened considerably. "That's right. I might as well give them a sporting chance.''

"That's very kind of you, Owen," Elizabeth said with a straight face. "Now, why don't you go and annoy the others with a bagpipe concert?''

CHAPTER

10

TRAVELER'S DIARY

Friday

Cameron is coming tomorrow. For the past three days the sea and sky have been an unbroken line of gray, barely visible through a curtain of rain. The air is wet and smells of salt and kelp, and I am chilled from the inside out. I do not think I am being very successful in my efforts to capture the spirit of the ancient island Celts, unless cabin fever was a problem in the Highlands. Unless one of them once wanted to stand out on the cliff in the rain screaming, "Get me off this island!"

Three days in a Nissen hut with these people . . . At least Owen has not played his bagpipes anymore. Denny has been teasing him about playing an American Indian rain dance by mistake, and saying that the rain is all Owen's fault. Owen sulked for most of the day, but since then most of his conversation has been about famous murderers, and he has been pumping the other diggers for their recollections about the cases. Of course, Denny instantly claimed to be one of them, which annoyed Owen still further, and the others made no secret of their disinterest. Actually, of course, no one remembers anything except in a vague jumble, the way we remember the Corn Laws, and I'm afraid Owen is becoming less popular by the minute. He is not the endearing sort of eccentric. He is a bit of a show-off.

Alasdair and Callum (true Scots?) profess not to be bothered by what they call "a little rain," and they spend much of the daylight hours out of the hut, supposedly tramping about the island. I suspect that Callum is exploring the sea cave. Alasdair seems to be indulging his preference for solitude as much as anything, although he does occasionally allow Gitte to go with him, for which I am grateful.

And I have spent most of the leisure time (apart from mapping and so on) as close to the camp stove as I can get, in a nonstop bridge game against Leath and Marchand. Denny overbids. He cannot seem to grasp the idea that the object of the game is to *win*.

Gitte talks incessantly, which she calls "practicing her English." I don't see why Alasdair doesn't just buy a cocker spaniel and be done with it! Why do some intelligent men like unintellectual women? Is it restful for their egos, or just an answer to the servant problem?

Thank God, I'll be seeing Cameron tomorrow. That thought has enabled me to be civil to everyone throughout this interminable downpour. Cameron seems so pleasant and normal, now that everyone else I know is grating on my nerves.

I am beginning to imagine this island in winter. No wonder the old Scots thought of hell as a cold, wet place. It must have been a grim life. It makes you understand why Celtic and Norse mythology is so pessimistic compared to Greek myths. The Northern people simply couldn't imagine a care-free existence, even for the gods.

I just wish the rain would stop.

By the wee hours on Friday morning the drumming of rain on the hut's tin roof had begun to subside, and when Elizabeth peeped out the door just past six, the sky was an encouraging shade of blue. She ran her hand through her jumble of curls, and hoped that one day would be enough time for the frizz to go away.

Denny Allan rounded the corner of the Nissen hut carrying two tin cups of spring water and Tang. "Pill time!" he announced.

Elizabeth took the cup and the capsule, trying to smile. She always felt like a gorgon in the morning, and she wished people wouldn't expect her to be civil before she had lipstick on. Some women could manage the disheveled look, she thought, but she was not among them.

"How's the hand today?" Denny asked.

Elizabeth gulped down her medicine. "Fine," she croaked. "I mean, it isn't infected, but the cut is rather deep. I suppose I could have used stitches, but I'm not very brave about things like that. Anyhow, I put a fresh bandage on it. Is anyone at the burn now? I want to wash up."

"I saw Callum, but he was about finished when I was there. Leath and Marchand have been up for ages, getting ready for today's project. Where's Alasdair?"

Elizabeth made a face. "He has also been up a while. He's

in there helping Gitte make breakfast, and she is simpering like mad.''

"Oh, well." Denny smiled. "You know how women are with a foreign boyfriend."

With that he strolled away, leaving Elizabeth to wonder whether or not she had been insulted.

Derek Marchand, delighted with the return of good weather, supervised the assembling of the surveying equipment for measuring the standing stones. As a civil engineer he was in his element with tachymeters and tripods. He had risen at dawn, and the traces of red on the horizon had lifted his spirits immeasurably. His first impulse had been to shake Tom Leath awake and to begin the day at once, but an instant later he decided that he did not want to share these early moments with anyone.

He pulled on a white fisherman's sweater over his turtleneck and set off inland toward the stones. The peat was still slippery from the previous rains, but to Marchand's nose the air smelled dry and fresh—a further promise that today the work would begin in earnest. The stones were still black shapes in the graying light of morning, and their twisted forms silhouetted against the sky looked oddly graceful, like dancers frozen in place. They seemed to bow to each other and to him, beckoning him closer.

Derek Marchand wondered what dawn it was, or perhaps what moonset, that would make the stones reveal their secret to a waiting communicant. Midsummer, perhaps, or Beltane. He was sure that there was some significance to the standing stones and that the paths of sun and moon were somehow bound to this ring of rock mired in peat on a forgotten island. If you stood just here—or perhaps there, by the tall tapered stone—and looked . . . where? At the mountain? At the smaller island just past the channel? . . . From some such point of reference, on a given day ordained centuries ago, the sun would rise just over one certain stone; or perhaps by standing at one special place within the circle, one could see the moon caught in a fold between two mountains.

The ancient engineers had set it all up to some heavenly purpose, and modern man had yet to determine what it was. Marchand was sure, though, that the extraordinary efforts put forth to construct that monument over a span of decades had not been expended frivolously or for the sake of art. There had been some careful plan at work, perhaps a religious one. He was certain that the circle had been precisely engineered to tell its builders something that they needed to know. The time of the solstice, perhaps, for planting or for worship. What in heaven—literally—had they watched for?

Such determinations were months—perhaps years—away from the work at hand. Before the astronomical significance of the Banrigh stones could be considered, hours of more prosaic measuring had to be done, in order to determine heights, widths, and angles. Marchand thought he might even leave the star-charting to a younger scholar. He doubted that he had the time or the strength to stay for all the answers. He would settle for his short-term goal: determining the unit of measurement they had depended on to construct their circle. That was knowledge enough for him. They had not been children, these old ones. For all their quaintness of dress and lifestyle (to modern sensibilities), Marchand did not underestimate them for a moment. Modern scientists achieved a good deal by standing on the shoulders of a host of others whose discoveries had made later ones possible, but these old ones had stood alone, and they had accomplished much.

He watched the sun come up over the water and shower the stones with golden light. Far off were wave sounds and the cry of seabirds, but across the stubble of heather, among the standing stones, all was quiet.

Two hours later the circle was glinting in bright sunshine, and the site was animated by the babble of voices and a flash of red and yellow sweatshirts weaving in and out among the stones.

Marchand, looking like a silver-haired gnome, was directing the bustle of activity, sending his workers scurrying to and fro with every new instruction. The first order of business was to check the temperature and the humidity, since weather conditions—especially dampness—affected the readings of the electronic surveying instrument.

Tom Leath, in a hangover-induced calm, was leaning against one of the stones, studying an ordnance map, trying to concentrate on Denny Allan's explanation of the procedure. Leath, who was accustomed neither to surveying nor to Scottish accents, and who was not in his most receptive mood at present, kept nodding and wishing that the lilting Glasgow accent would stop clanging in his head.

"The ordnance survey has the national grid superimposed on it, right?" Denny was saying. "Okay, in the margin you'll find the angle between grid north and true north . . . Not following me? Look, if we calculate the azimuth of a line with respect to the grid, it can be reduced to true north if we apply the correction obtained at the observer's end of the line. And if we know the grid coordinates of two points, then we can find the azimuth of the line joining the two points.''

"Fine with me." Leath shrugged. "We tend to put things in simpler terms for the measuring done in my fieldwork."

Denny smiled. "I know you'll be wanting to get on to your own specialty here."

"Right. Give me a kitchen midden. Once I find where these fellows dumped their garbage, I can find out where they lived."

"There's a lot of peat covering up that secret."

"Too right." Leath sighed. "It took a major storm on Mainland in the Orkneys to uncover the ruins at Skara Brae. I suppose I could pray for more rain. Ah, well, that's neither here nor there. Suppose you tell me in less grandiose terms how I can help."

Denny handed the Englishman a hexagonal-shaped prism. "Hold this," he said. "And go and stand where I tell you."

The site may have been ancient, but the surveying techniques were not. The tachymeter used an infrared beam bounced off the prism to determine distance, and Leath's job was to hold the prism against the base of each standing stone while Denny took aim from the tripod set up in center circle.

"We are closing a traverse," Denny said to Elizabeth, who was noting down the figures on a clipboard as he called them out to her.

"Shall I write that down?" Elizabeth asked.

"No, hen, I'm explaining it to you. Closing a traverse means that we will be shooting the location of a number of points around a circle and then coming back to our original point."

"Impressive jargon," Elizabeth said approvingly. "Mind if I take a look through the sight?"

Denny stepped back and motioned her to the tachymeter. "No! Don't stand with your legs astraddle the tripod legs, dear! It's too easy to bump it out of alignment that way. Stand between the legs. That's fine. Now have a look."

She peered into the lens. "It's upside down," she announced.

"It's supposed to be."

"I see a little symbol on the stick. I think it's supposed to be a V."

"That stands for five," Denny told her. "They put it in Roman numerals so you won't mistake it for a nine when you see it upside down."

"Why don't you just hold the measuring stick upside down?" Elizabeth wanted to know.

Denny shook his head. "There's no explaining science to some people," he said.

"That means you haven't a clue." Elizabeth nodded.

The day spent measuring the circle was the most perfect one imaginable in a Highland summer: comfortably warm sunshine and a bright blue sky with only a few puffs of clouds low on the horizon. They had spent many hours carefully measuring the site and rechecking their findings, stopping only for quick lunch of potted meat sandwiches fetched to the site by Alasdair, who was being more cooperative than anyone had expected. He and Gitte had taken charge of a second tripod and were measuring the levels at the base of each stone, while Owen followed, making chalk marks on the stones to indicate the points of measurement. Callum, as usual, photographed the work in progress.

Marchand and Denny had compared their findings and pronounced the site a flattened circle, composed of two arcs of 240 degrees and 120 degrees respectively.

"Does that make sense?" Elizabeth wanted to know; she was resting on the grass, adding notations to her clipboard.

"I think so," said Owen, who was also resting. "There are hundreds of these stone circles all over Britain, and from what Marchand was saying today, that seems to be one of the recognized types of circles."

"I haven't seen any evidence of a tomb, yet, have you?"

"I asked about that," Owen said. "Callum told me that if you do find tombs associated with stone circles, they were added by a later culture. The original builders did not use the circles for burial purposes."

"So much for the treasure." Elizabeth sighed. "I wondered when I saw Alasdair poking into the peat with a sharp stick. What was he looking for?"

Owen shrugged. "More stones. They seem to think a few are missing."

"The villagers probably snatched them for millstones in the Middle Ages."

"It's really going to be difficult to measure that outer ring of the henge monument. The posts were usually timber or small stones, and those will be a couple of feet into the turf by now."

Elizabeth nodded. "Shoveling required. I doubt if we get to that stage on this expedition, though. If we stay that long, we'll be digging peat anyway—to burn!"

* * *

They kept working until seven to make up for the days the rain had cost them. Even then the sky was bright with full sun, but everyone except Marchand was too tired to care. He and Denny stayed at the circle for "just one more measuring," while the others straggled off to the burn to wash off the sweat before going back to camp.

Elizabeth shivered as she plunged her arms into the icy spring. "Ugh!" she said. "The Bronze Age is losing its charm incredibly fast."

Gitte nodded. "Tonight I will heat water on the camping stove, no matter how long it takes. I do not think we get really clean in cold water."

"Boil some extra water," Owen told her. "I'll want some to soften up my honey and hot wax."

"You'll crack the jar," Gitte told him.

Owen rolled his eyes. "I'll wait until it cools off some. Honestly!"

"So you're cleaning the bagpipes tonight, huh, Owen?" Elizabeth asked.

He blushed. "I might as well. You'll be playing bridge, and nobody else wants to talk to me. Besides, Marchand says that he's sending me over to the small island to measure that stone tomorrow, now that it's stopped raining. I told him I'd just take some food and camp over there for a couple of days. That way I can play my bagpipes without disturbing anyone."

Elizabeth privately thought that sound would carry very well indeed over still water, but she decided not to say so. Perhaps Owen wanted her to protest that his playing was no disturbance at all, and that was nearly true. It was not that he played well, but it took enormous lung power to play, and

113

as a relative beginner, Owen had very little endurance. He was, therefore, only able to be a nuisance for short periods of time.

By the time Marchand and Denny showed up, tripods slung over their shoulders, there were long shadows in the grass and the air was chilly. Gitte had finished boiling the water on the camping stove and had allowed its burners to be used for preparing dinner, a concoction of stewed vegetables in beef broth. True to his word, Owen had commandeered a tin cup full of the water and had set his wax-and-honey mixture in it to reach the proper consistency for lubrication.

"You might have saved some of it for coffee!" Alasdair had grumbled, so Gitte had gone back to the spring for more water. She then set a smaller pan to boil.

Marchand, his cheeks red from sun and exercise, accepted a steaming cup of tea and took his place at the long table beside Callum, who was eating cheese and crackers while he waited for the stew. "What did you think of your day, then?" he asked heartily.

Among the assorted murmurs of enthusiasm, Owen piped up. "I was still hoping we'd find a burial chamber."

Callum looked up from his cracker. "Do you want neolithic, or will any one do?"

Owen narrowed his eyes. "I don't mean the village cemetery, thank you!"

Denny laughed. "I don't think that's what he meant, Owen! You're talking about the sea dead, aren't you?"

Callum nodded. "Yes, of course. I took some photos of them, but of course they aren't germane to the project."

Owen was instantly alert. "Sea burial?"

"Those flat stones near the causeway. The ones sticking

114

up in the ground, like small standing stones. The islanders put them there. It's the way they buried bodies washed ashore from shipwrecks. They didn't do crosses, because they didn't know if the deceased were Christian or not."

"You mustn't disturb them, though," Tom Leath warned him. "That crosses the line between archaeology and grave robbing. They're much too recent to interest us anyway."

Alasdair yawned and stretched. "Owen won't do any body snatching, will you, Owen? There's no sport in it. I fancy there's another site on the island as well. Did you catch that, Farthing?"

Callum shrugged. "The Tarans, you mean? It's possible, I suppose. I haven't looked closely."

Owen, who had fished the jar of honey and hot wax out of the pan of water, looked up from his bagpipes. "What are *Tarans*?" he demanded.

"Unbaptized children. When a child was stillborn, or if it died before it could be given the rite of baptism, the islanders did not bury it in the ordinary cemetery."

"They were put in unmarked graves in special burial grounds high up in the hills or on the grassy ledges of cliffs facing the sea," Alasdair said in a tone that made it clear that he was showing off rather than being helpful.

"Why?" asked Elizabeth, whose passion for folklore had been aroused by the discussion.

"To give them a chance at salvation," Callum said solemnly. "The high places are halfway between heaven and earth, and their parents hoped that the kind spirits of the middle kingdom—between heaven and hell—would take pity on the little spirits."

"They say that you can hear the wee things crying in the wind," said Alasdair, smirking at Elizabeth's tears.

"And there's such a place here on Banrigh?" Owen asked. He was carefully pouring the thick mixture into the sac of his bagpipes, but he was paying careful attention to the conversation nonetheless.

"Perhaps," Alasdair said, with a mocking smile. "I thought I might go off and see tomorrow. *By myself*," he added to the three pairs of pleading eyes gazing hopefully at him.

"I couldn't go anyway." Owen shrugged. "Tomorrow I'm taking the boat to the little island." He sloshed his instrument around a bit in order to coat the inside thoroughly. "I'll let it sit for a bit before I dump it out," he said to no one in particular.

"I couldn't go tomorrow, either," Elizabeth said proudly. "Cameron is coming, you know."

"I'd leave the place alone, Alasdair, if I were you," said Callum. "It'll bring you no luck."

Alasdair smirked. "People make their own luck, I always think!"

CHAPTER

11

Alasdair looked with disfavor at the breakfast foods haphazardly laid out on the slightly sticky wooden table. This must be someone's idea of working-class Scout fare: lardlike margarine, aging bread, teabags, and a cracked cup of white sugar. Powdered orange juice, stewed tomatoes, and canned beans would no doubt follow. He shuddered, wondering if he ought to demand that a supply of stomach tablets to be added to whatever the biologist would be asked to bring on his next stopover. He decided against it. If he complained, the others might think him not a team player, which of course he wasn't. He thought teamwork was a peculiar form of stupidity, merely sharing the incompetence so that no one could be blamed when things went wrong. Alasdair, who could be chillingly efficient when he chose to be, had no use for the encumbrance of others when he wanted to get something done.

He searched about in the larder for the cheese. That and

the bread would make a barely acceptable breakfast, he decided, and he could eat it quickly, without having to be bothered by the insipid chatter of the others. He glanced over at Gitte, who was still sleeping. She was a stupid cow, of course; he'd never met a woman who wasn't, only some who thought they weren't. He wondered why women made such a virtue of self-sacrifice; perhaps it was nature's way of making it easy to exploit them.

He stood up. Time to get moving. There would be reproachful looks and sniffles of martyrdom to endure when he got back, but Gitte was used to being left out when it suited him, and well she knew that sulking would get her nowhere. Still, he preferred to deal with her later, rather than now.

He didn't want to miss the biologist, though. That was important. Hastily, he scribbled a note:

> Must see C. Dawson when he arrives. I want to send something back with him. Also have instructions regarding soil samples, etc. Do not let him leave until I return.
>
> A. McEwan.

That should do it, he thought to himself. It left no room for argument. He anchored the note to the table with a corner of the sugar cup; then he pulled on his anorak. He had better be off before the others woke—lazy pigs!

Elizabeth tugged on her cleanest lambswool pullover—the burgundy-colored one that set off her dark hair so nicely. She wished she had brought a fourth pair of jeans, but perhaps it

118

wouldn't have mattered. The cold spring water was not able to get them really clean anyway, and it took them days and days to dry in the moist chill of a Highland summer.

Elizabeth reached for a paper tissue and stifled a sneeze. She was running low on tissues; she must remember to ask Cameron to bring her some. Perhaps this was the beginning of a cold. She wouldn't be surprised, considering the climate. She had almost forgotten what it felt like not to be cold and slightly damp. Did her ancestors really need a marauding English army to persuade them to emigrate? The very thought of winter would have sent her packing. It's all a matter of what you're used to, though, she told herself. Only she and Owen, the Americans, seemed to notice the cold. Gitte wore a T-shirt most of the time and seemed to think the weather was normal.

Still, it was beautiful in the Highlands. She thought that if one had a little house in some less remote place—like Skye—with central heating and a generous supply of hot water, Scotland could be a wonderful place in which to live. However, if one had to subsist in a tin shack from World War II, with no conveniences and nothing to eat but carbohydrates, one might as well be a seal.

She distracted herself with the thought that Cameron was coming in a matter of hours, and for that momentous occasion she decided to heat a pan of water on the camp stove. She would try to get her face and hands *really* clean.

Owen Gilchrist gave his bagpipes a final swish for good measure and then carefully poured the mixture into the ground behind the hut. He had poured out the honey-and-hot-wax mixture the night before, according to the instructions; after he had kneaded the leather bag to make sure that the inside was entirely lubricated, he had set the bag upside down on the grass to drain. This morning he had used some of the hot water to swish it out one last time. The directions hadn't said to do this, but he thought it seemed like a good idea. He'd added half a cup of warm water to the bagpipe through the blowpipe and then quickly dumped it out. It hadn't taken much. There was still enough water in the pan on the stove to make a few cups of tea, when it eventually boiled, especially since Alasdair seemed to have skipped out without breakfast. Owen felt that this was an insult directed at him personally, but from the way the Danish girl was sniffling while she worked, perhaps the snub had been general.

He thought he might not wait for Elizabeth's boyfriend to arrive. It wasn't as if he were bringing mail or candy bars or anything worth waiting for. He might as well get Callum to help him haul the boat out of the cave. He could set off for the little island right away.

It was while he was blowing a few experimental notes on the newly cleaned pipes that Owen remembered that there was something Cameron could bring that would interest him. News. If the Edinburgh police had apprehended Keenan's murderer, surely the news would be all over the newspapers and radio. Assuming, of course, that Cameron had bothered to listen. Still, he'd better hang around and ask him; certainly no one else would bother to do so, and he couldn't stand the suspense another week. He continued to reassemble his pipes, fantasizing happily about his murder theory being proved right, and the others all begging his pardon for teasing him. He allowed himself to manufacture these small scenes of triumph to make up for the fact that in real life they never, ever happened.

Gitte stared at the tin plate of powdered eggs slowly congealing in front of her. Where was everybody this morning? It was only half past eight, and only the two Americans were to be found. She supposed that Marchand had paid an early visit to the site, taking Leath, and probably Denny, with him.

She didn't want to think about Alasdair just then, because that would make the tears come. She wished she could ask the American girl how she managed to get on so well with her Scottish boyfriend, but perhaps it was early days yet. Anyway, Gitte did not feel like confiding in Elizabeth, who acted altogether too much like one of the men, if you asked her.

"Here," she said grudgingly, pushing the plate of eggs toward Elizabeth. "You might as well have these."

"No, thank you," Elizabeth said with equal insincerity. "I'm sure that they can be reheated." *Perhaps Alasdair will choke on them,* she thought spitefully. She picked up the pill that Denny had left her and swallowed it with the last bit of her tea.

"Do you plan to stay here all day waiting for your boyfriend?" Gitte asked with more than a hint of scorn.

Elizabeth was stung. "I guess not!" she snapped. "What about you?"

Gitte began clearing the breakfast things from the table. "I have work to do. They will need me at the site."

Elizabeth left the Nissen hut, but she did not go straight to the standing stones. *Perhaps he is already on his way,* she thought, *and I can catch a glimpse of the boat.* She had stood

121

on the cliff for several minutes, shivering in a sharp sea wind, before she realized that he would probably be coming to the other side of the island, as he had the time before. The wind in the rocks did sound a bit like a baby's cry, she thought. That was probably the origin of the Taran legends. The sky was gunmetal-gray, but there was no hint of rain, and no darker clouds on the horizon, so she supposed that he would still be coming.

A movement on the beach below caught her eye, and she saw the seal—perhaps the one Denny had told her about—sitting on a flat rock near the shore. It was a deep, shiny brown, almost the color of the wet rock, and it seemed to be looking back at her. Around its neck she could see a bit of plastic that must be the radio collar. She thought of going to get her camera, but that would mean returning to the hut for another confrontation with Gitte, so she decided against it. She would settle for telling Cameron about it when he arrived. Or perhaps it would still be there then. She wondered if anyone would mind if she fed it. But fed it what? Did they eat anything besides raw fish? She must remember to ask Cameron.

Cameron Dawson had got a late start from the research station, so that it was nearly noon by the time he saw the mountains of Banrigh appear before him on the horizon. He had not quite liked the look of the sky, so he had stopped for one last check on the weather before setting out, in case the forecast had changed from the night before. It had not. A slow drizzle toward late afternoon was the worst he could expect, if the weather people were to be believed. He supposed he would have set off anyhow. Elizabeth was bound to take it personally if he did not turn up. She would excuse nothing less than a howling gale without doubting his devotion.

Probably she thought that he was a much better sailor than he was. It fit his Scottish image in her mind: a race of Highland fishermen. But Cameron, who had admittedly become more accustomed to boats while getting a degree in marine biology, was not used to manning the vessel alone. He usually had the company of two or three more experienced people, and their trips were either short ones, or else taken on much larger vessels than this that were professionally manned. He supposed that he had agreed to run supplies for her dig partly to ensure her acceptance on the crew and partly to impress her. But, of course, she wasn't impressed. She simply took these things for granted. He supposed that might be a compliment, in a way, except that she would have thought the same of every other Scot.

He wondered if he ought to have a go at landing on the western side of the island, thus braving the rocky inlet; but another glance at the sky convinced him that this was not the day for heroics. He could feel the pitch of the sea beneath him, and knew that while this was by no means stormy weather, neither was it dead calm.

He wondered how Elizabeth was adjusting to life in the rough. No, he knew full well how she'd be taking it; what he wondered was whether she would admit it. He had brought her a tin of powdered cocoa mix and a box of chocolates as consolation, and he had firmly resolved to be as vague as possible about the comforts of his own research station. Hot water, he sensed, could easily be a source of hostility.

The island was quite near now. Time to begin maneuvering to land. Cameron suddenly wondered if everything was all right on Banrigh, but he had no idea why such a thought should have occurred to him.

Derek Marchand looked up from the theodolite, because he could no longer see the hexagonal prism in the viewfinder. He squinted at the dark stone for a moment. Finally, he caught sight of the reflector lying in the dirt in front of the stone. Elizabeth, who had been holding it, was running across the field toward a tall young man that for a moment he took to be Alasdair. That did not seem to make sense, and then he realized that this was the day the biologist was coming to see them, that, in fact, he had arrived.

Marchand consulted his watch. "Half twelve," he said to no one in particular. "I suppose we could break for lunch now." If it were up to him, he would have kept working; they had lost a good bit of time to the rain, and there was no saying they wouldn't lose even more. Still, he thought, he could probably use a break more than the young people. He was beginning to feel the chill in his bones now, and he tired more easily than he remembered. Years of relative inactivity had taken their toll, and he had only been able to get back into fieldwork when his wife had finally died. He felt guilty putting it like that, but he assured himself that it did not mean he didn't miss her, only that he was adjusting well by taking up new interests. In fact, he hardly thought of her at all anymore, but he told himself that this was better than the vague sense of annoyance she had stirred in him while she was alive. Once he had caught himself wondering if she would have come with him on a dig the way these young girls did today, but he could not decide about that. Except for a few random images that seemed like, and probably were, snapshots in the family album, he had no memory of her youth. She had just been there, he supposed, while his preoccupation was with himself, his career, and the war.

He looked at the plump American girl embracing her young man, and they were as foreign to him as fifth-century Celts.

Elizabeth understood that her time alone with Cameron would have to wait until he chatted with all the other diggers, received lists of supplies they needed and items they wanted sent back to the mainland, and until he had a general visit with Denny and Marchand, probably over lunch. She had resigned herself to this delay, resolving not to compete for his attention like a neglected child, and not to brood on questions like whether or not he had missed her. In order not to seem impatient for this general socializing to end, she paid considerably more attention to her potted meat sandwich than it merited.

She sat down on a rock very close to Cameron, thinking that she could at least allow herself to be this proprietary. He smiled at her, and then turned back to his conversation with Denny, who was just telling him about the Banrigh seal.

"I saw it, too!" Elizabeth cried, forgetting her resolution about Cameron's attention.

"Then I suppose I can believe you, Denny," Cameron said solemnly. "One of our seals frequents your island. I'll see if I can figure out which one he is when I get back."

Owen appeared just then, red faced and panting. "We've been getting the boat out, Callum and I, but I wanted to see you before I left. Might as well eat, too," he added. "My provisions are already packed up."

"Owen will be staying a couple of nights on the small island to study the menhir there," Elizabeth explained.

Owen did not look pleased at the prospect. "It's awfully gloomy today," he said, frowning up at the sky. "Did you run into rain?"

"No," said Cameron. "But there may be some later on. You'll want to set off soon. It's not dead calm as it is."

Owen looked as if he would like to say something else on the subject, but instead he asked, "Have they found the Edinburgh killer yet?"

"I don't think so," Cameron replied. "It hasn't been mentioned on any news broadcasts."

Owen looked pleased. He turned away and began to make himself a sandwich without even so much as a thank-you.

"Owen," Denny said, "just how much boating experience have you had anyway?"

"None," Owen said, smearing meat paste on a wedge of bread.

Callum Farthing looked up. "None?"

Owen flushed. "Well, it isn't far! Three-quarters of a mile at the most."

"It will seem far if a storm comes in," said Denny. "Then how will you get back?"

Callum sighed and stood up. "I suppose I'd better take him over."

"But I'll be stranded!" Owen cried. "What if I run out of food or something?"

Denny smirked. "You're taking your bagpipes, aren't you, lad? If you want to come back, give us a shout."

"I was planning on playing while I was over there," said Owen. "How will you know which is which?"

Callum shrugged. "Can you play taps? You wouldn't be likely to practice that tune, would you? Play that when you want to be brought back."

"Okay," Owen mumbled. "I guess it's better than getting swept away in that dinky boat." Another thought struck him. "Are you sure you'll be able to hear me from here?"

Denny sighed. "I'm afraid so, Owen."

Callum and Owen said their goodbyes to the group and headed for the beach where they had left the boat. For the rest of lunch Marchand explained what they had been doing on the dig, and he and Leath discussed the various things that needed to be sent back to the mainland: Callum's film, Alasdair's soil samples.

"Talking of Alasdair, where is he?" asked Denny. "Didn't you say he left a note saying he needed to see Cameron?"

Elizabeth nodded. "Yes. He left it quite early. Before he went to look for his Tarans." She made a face.

"His what?" asked Cameron.

Elizabeth shook her head. "Cultural illiteracy strikes again."

"They're burial grounds up on cliffs," Denny told him. "Nothing you'd have come across in Auld Reekie."

Gitte, who had said almost nothing since Cameron's arrival, looked worried. "Has no one seen him today?"

"I'm sure he's fine," Denny said automatically, but he looked at Cameron as he said it, and his eyes were grave.

Cameron stood up. "Perhaps we ought to go and hunt him up," he said with careful heartiness. "I'm sure he just lost track of the time, but we'd better find him if he wants a word with me before I leave. Let's spread out, shall we? Elizabeth, want to come with me?''

Elizabeth realized at once that this was to be their time together, and while she would have preferred another way to spend it, she could hardly say so, with everyone so concerned about Alasdair—but pretending not to be. They started off together up the path that led through the hills and, eventually, back to where Cameron had left his boat. The others had started out in different directions along the cliffs to search the edges of the island.

Elizabeth looked out at the peat bogs, now a dull green in the gray light of an overcast sky. The black speckled rocks dotted the field like birds' eggs. What color had Alasdair been wearing? Would he be easy to spot? Should they call out to him?

"I cut my finger," she said, in consequence of nothing.

After a moment's pause, Cameron replied, "I'm sorry. Is it painful?"

"A little," Elizabeth said, glad she could say that it was. "I keep the bandage changed, and Denny has given me some of his antibiotics—just in case."

"You shouldn't . . ." *Take other people's medicine*, Cameron was going to say, but he realized that she might take this as a lack of concern for her. There might have been a small chance of infection, after all, so what did it matter if she took a few pills. "You shouldn't try to use it too much," he finished.

She nodded. "I'll be careful. I always wash my hands after I've been working."

"I brought you a few things," he said, fishing a package

out of the pocket of his anorak. "Chocolate bars and some cocoa. You look as if you need a treat."

The spark in Elizabeth's eyes made him realize that this had been an unwise thing to say, but he thought that a manufactured excuse might make things worse, so he said nothing.

"Thank you," she said at last. "I promise to share them round."

"Have you missed me?"

Elizabeth was grateful that he had posed the question before she burst out with it. "I expect I have," she replied. "It's hard to say, really. Things are so primitive here, and practically everyone is so difficult, that I can't tell if I miss you desperately, or if I'd just be glad to see anybody who isn't on this dig!"

"We'll hope it's more than that," said Cameron.

"Well, I wouldn't want you getting too conceited."

Cameron looked at the rocks on one side of the path, and at the sheer drop on the other. "Why did Alasdair go looking for this Taran place?"

"Chiefly to taunt Owen, I think," Elizabeth said. "He's a great one for solitude, is Alasdair—always going off by himself anyway. Having spent a week with Gitte, I can't say that I blame him. And he has been teasing Owen about his morbid tastes in crime and about his image of archaeology as a child's treasure hunt. I think he wanted to drive Owen mad with envy by suggesting that he had made a discovery concerning one or both."

"Suppose he has?"

"I don't think so," said Elizabeth. "I don't think he'd want to give Owen the satisfaction of being proved right. It would almost be like Alasdair to cover up anything interesting, just for spite."

Cameron considered this. "I suppose the Crown would get anything they found anyway. Isn't that how it works?"

Elizabeth stared at him. "Don't you know? It's *your* country!"

"Well, they've never asked me for any seals. I thought the subject might have come up, what with you being archaeologists and all."

"I'm an anthropologist," Elizabeth reminded him. "And the Queen is welcome to any old bones I find. Actually, I think the stuff gets claimed for the Crown as a technicality, but in fact it would end up in a museum somewhere. Probably Edinburgh, like the St. Ninian's treasure."

Cameron nodded. "Very likely."

"But there isn't anything to find, of course. Tarans are unbaptized babies buried in unmarked graves. They wouldn't be buried with anything at all. Even the bones may be dust by now. I tell you, all this is Alasdair's idea of a joke." She shivered. "I have missed you. Denny is nice enough in his shallow little way, but sometimes I just want to talk to you so much . . ."

Cameron wasn't listening. He stared ahead at nothing, one ear cocked in the direction of the cliff. After a moment's pause, Elizabeth heard it too. The echo of a scream that could only be Gitte, followed by shouts for help.

Cameron said, "They've found Alasdair."

CHAPTER

12

"He's going to be all right," Denny kept saying, although no one was listening. He was not sure what to do, but it seemed to him that being cheerful and encouraging was both innocuous and satisfying. He had no idea whether or not it was true, but it seemed the proper attitude to take.

Denny and Gitte had been the first ones to find Alasdair, as he lay unconscious but still breathing at the base of a rocky hill, his head just to the left of a white-flecked stone that must have stopped his fall. A smear of dirt and a long scratch on his cheek were the only signs of injury, but they knew that he must have hit the back of his head on the rock and that they must not move him. Denny remembered reading that somewhere.

After the one involuntary scream, Gitte had not uttered another sound. Denny shouted for help, his hands cupped against his cheeks, as he scanned the cliffs for a glimpse of the others. Gitte sat down on the ground beside Alasdair, never taking her eyes off his face, watching to see that his shallow breathing did not stop.

After a long few minutes, Derek Marchand and Tom Leath appeared, working their way down a grassy slope from the other direction. Leath bent over the body, taking Alasdair's wrist between his fingers. "What did you do?" he asked.

"Nothing!" Denny said, as if that were a virtue.

"Should we radio for help?" asked Marchand, kneeling on the other side of Alasdair. "Perhaps an emergency helicopter?"

"No," said Leath. "Our radio isn't strong enough. We can just reach the next island. Trust the medic to be the first casualty!"

"I suppose we'll have to get Dawson to take him off by boat, then. He's still here, is he not?"

Denny caught sight of Cameron's red anorak on the path above them. "He's just coming now!"

Leath glanced at Denny. "We need blankets from camp to cover him up. I expect he's in shock. Is there anything in the medical kit that would help? I suppose not. These scratches aren't serious."

"When we get on the boat, I will clean them," Gitte said calmly. "I am going with him."

Denny ended the silence that followed. "Well . . . right," he said. "I'm off to fetch the blankets."

Marchand didn't quite like the paleness of Alasdair's face—although it was a better face now that the scornful look was gone. He looked much younger somehow. "Should we make a stretcher of some sort?"

Leath shrugged. "From what? It might be better to waste no time. Just carry him to the boat as carefully as we can."

Marchand looked up at the lowering sky. "I hope the weather holds."

Elizabeth and Cameron spent their last few minutes together clearing space in the cabin of the boat for Alasdair. They found a stack of white woolen blankets in the chest with the life preservers, and Elizabeth was spreading them out on the floor, smoothing out the creases as best she could. Cameron was looking at sea charts. "I suppose I could make for Skye," he murmured, tracing his finger along the map. "But it's twice as far, and there's no hospital there. I think there's one on Lewis, but if he's badly hurt, he ought to go to Inverness anyway."

Elizabeth nodded, still smoothing blankets. "When will you be back?"

"Next Saturday," said Cameron. "I really can't come any sooner! I have to go to the mainland for supplies, and I expect I'll look in at hospital and see how Alasdair is doing. I need to get some work done on my project this week as well. I simply haven't time."

Elizabeth said nothing. She seemed intent on her work, but he could tell from the stiffness of her movements that she was listening.

"Of course, if there's an emergency, you can always call me on the radio."

"Not much chance for intimate conversation there," she said lightly.

"No. I am sorry. I know you're upset. And, of course, worried about Alasdair."

Elizabeth shrugged. Being worried about Alasdair might have been preferable to the guilt she felt for her slight concern. When she did not like a person, no misfortune that befell him could make her like him any better. "I hope he isn't seriously hurt," she said carefully.

"He shouldn't have gone climbing those cliffs alone."

"That was the whole point of it, Cameron," Elizabeth said. "Alasdair liked being alone, and he liked leaving people out of things. I think secrets made him feel superior. That's probably why he was studying medicine."

Cameron grinned in spite of himself. "You'll be all right here, won't you?"

"I suppose so. I'm coming down with a cold. Will you bring me some tissues?"

"I'll put them on the list." A movement up the hill caught Cameron's attention. "Here they come, Elizabeth. Gitte seems to be coming with him—she's carrying her duffel bag."

Elizabeth got to her feet and slid her hand into Cameron's. "Leath and Denny are carrying Alasdair. He's still unconscious."

"It was a bad fall," Cameron said. "I wonder how he lost his balance."

Elizabeth watched the silent procession make its way toward the boat. "I wonder if he did," she said.

"And then there were five," Denny said, as they walked back to the stone circle.

Elizabeth frowned. "Five?"

"You, me, Callum, Leath, and Derek Marchand. I'm not counting Owen until he comes back day after tomorrow."

"We'll manage," said Elizabeth. "I can hold the prism *and* do the chalk marks."

"I know. Certainly Alasdair and Gitte were more expendable than, say, Callum and I. Bad luck for him, taking a fall like that. Head injuries are funny things. I've known people knocked out like that who came to ten minutes later and went right about their business.''

"I thought we might try to get Cameron on the radio tomorrow night and see what news he has of Alasdair. No, he said he's going to the mainland after supplies. The night after, then."

"Alasdair might be ready to come back by midweek," Denny said, "Unless he's one of the self-dramatizing types."

"Cameron said he isn't coming back until Saturday," Elizabeth said.

"Well, he's a very serious sort, is Cameron. He was always at the books at Fettes. Looked a bit like an owl in those days. Big glasses. Funny haircut. Terminal case of adolescence."

"He has improved considerably since then," said Elizabeth.

"Yes. I was very relieved to find that you weren't a seal or a porpoise," he told her. "Cameron has indeed progressed."

"I wish I understood him better. Sometimes I think that the British and the Americans do *not* speak the same language."

"So Cameron was telling me. When he first began driving in Virginia, he saw a sign that said DRIVE ON THE PAVEMENT . . . something like that. Well, of course, in Scotland the pavement is the sidewalk. He thought they were mad."

"It isn't only that. You can learn that a jumper is a sweater, and a banger is a sausage, and that a trunk call means long distance. Even Americans have different names for things.

Try ordering a hoagie in New York sometime. But there are cultural differences that you don't learn, because you don't know they're there.''

Denny looked puzzled. "Like what?"

"I don't know." Elizabeth sighed. "I told you: I don't know they're there. I just feel it."

The mood for the remainder of the day was subdued. When Callum returned, they told him about the accident in brief, understated terms, and he nodded and said that it was unfortunate. Derek Marchand, leaning on the surveying staff and looking a bit like Moses, made a little speech to the effect that while their thoughts were with Alasdair, they ought to continue with the work at hand, that Alasdair would want it that way, and so on. Everyone listened politely; no one had anything to add, and work went on as usual, despite a sharp wind from the darkening sky.

"I should have been an Egyptologist," Tom Leath thought for the hundredth time.

"Is Owen settled in on the island all right?" Elizabeth asked Callum.

"He has everything he needs," Callum said. I let him take my one-man tent. A few cold meals won't hurt him."

"Can we see him from the cliffs?"

"No. His camp is on the other side, where the shore is open for landing. He didn't want to carry his things too far from that."

"Good," said Denny, who had stopped to listen. "If we're lucky, the hills will muffle the sound of his piping."

Callum smiled and began to adjust the lens on his camera.

"Do you think we ought to tell him about Alasdair?" Elizabeth asked.

Denny gave her a sour smile. "Let's save it for a surprise when he comes back."

The rain came by late evening, so that it was impossible to tell when the day's dark clouds turned into an overcast night. Elizabeth lay huddled in her sleeping bag, the cold making her feel even more alone, and listened to the soft thud of rain on the tin cylinder. She was thinking about Cameron, in a sort of backward rehearsal of all the things she could have said, but she kept thinking about old war movies from the Forties, the ones where the handsome American pilot falls in love with an English girl. They always had chestnut brown hair, these English girls (even in black and white you could tell), and sweet soprano voices, and they always wore head scarfs. Sensible. Ordinary. Wholesome. Perfect noses. Elizabeth knew for a fact that she looked like a pumpkin in a head scarf. She didn't think she was reassuringly ordinary, either, not that she was to blame for that. Southerners are not known for being wholesome or ordinary. Too much imagination, she thought. I could be a quiet, sensible girl who'd be perfectly happy staying home and baking bread and weeding the garden. If I had a lobotomy, she thought grimly. She wondered just who it was that Cameron actually wanted, and if she had a chance of being that person.

For a moment, as she closed her eyes, she thought she heard the wail of Owen's bagpipes, but it might have been the wind.

Sunday was cloudy and dark, but the rain held off until early evening, so that they were able to get much work done at the site. Elizabeth thought that it went more smoothly with fewer people jostling each other about. She was becoming much more experienced at surveying now, and since it seemed certain that there would be no work in her own specialty to keep her busy, she had to make herself useful in other ways.

She missed Cameron very much. His brief visit the day before, attended by so much chaos, was worse than no visit at all. Even communication by radio had been denied her because the weather Sunday night was not good, and, in her opinion, Tom Leath was too lazy to make the effort to try to raise the other island in difficult broadcasting conditions. Even her protests of concern for Alasdair (more useful than true) had been met with a shrug and Leath's opinion that it was too soon to learn much anyhow. He'd try Monday night,

138

he said, even if the weather had not let up, and Elizabeth had to be content with that.

On Monday it had rained off and on most of the day, but they had worked anyway. Marchand was anxious to get the major portion of the measuring finished in case a real storm appeared. Elizabeth listened off and on during the day for the sound of bagpipes from the smaller island, half expecting to hear taps sounded in screeching desperation. Surely Owen must be chilled and tired of cold food by now, she thought. He had been working alone there for two days and a half. She decided that he had more endurance than she had given him credit for, but she doubted that he was taking it in cheerful pioneer spirit. She had not heard his bagpipes since his first night over there. Either he was playing quietly, or—as she suspected—he was sulking in his tent with his murder books.

On her trips from the Nissen hut to the stone circle, she had once or twice seen the seal, but she had not caught a glimpse of Owen at work on the menhir on the smaller island. If, as she suspected, he was refusing to work during drizzle, he might be there a long time completing his work. She suspected that the prospect of more days in an unheated tent, with canned food, would persuade him to brave the elements.

When about five o'clock Monday evening the drizzle turned into a downpour, she even began to feel sorry for Owen. "Aren't you going to go and get him, Callum?"

He squinted at her through wet eyelashes. "What? In this muck? By tomorrow it may clear off."

"It may also get worse," Elizabeth pointed out.

"Aye, but he hasn't signaled for us to come and get him."

"We haven't heard him," Denny said. "You know fine we spend most of our time out here at the circle, Callum. I doubt we'd hear him here."

"Go and get him, Callum," Elizabeth said. "He needs a hot meal at least. If he isn't finished, you can always send him back."

"All right!" said Callum. "And you're wanting me to go before supper, too, I suppose."

Elizabeth nodded. "If you wouldn't mind," she said politely, because she was sure that the matter was settled.

They trooped back to camp across the soggy peat fields, with the wind blowing a steady stream of water in their faces. "What you need is a nice cup of tea!" Denny shouted, nudging her arm.

"Right! I'm going to pour it over my head!" Elizabeth shouted back, pulling her rain hood tighter about her face. It was no use. She was soaked to the cervical vertebrae, she thought.

"Well, this is a nasty evening!" Derek Marchand announced when they were inside the Nissen hut. "I'm thinking we all ought to bunk in here for the night, or be drowned in our beds."

"It'll be a bit crowded," Tom Leath said, "but I'll take crowded over wet any day."

"Do you think you can raise anyone on the radio in this storm?" Marchand asked.

Leath shrugged. "I'll have a go at it after dinner."

"Good idea. Poor Callum, having to put out to sea in this, but I suppose we couldn't leave the American boy over there alone."

Elizabeth, who was brewing tea, smiled to herself. If it hadn't been for me, you would have, she thought. She began to take packets of dried-noodle dinners out of the supply box, calculating how many she would need to feed six people, and how much water that would require. A sudden sound carried on the wind made her look up from her task. "That's odd," she said. "Hasn't Callum left already?"

"Three quarters of an hour ago, at least," Denny said. "Why?"

"Just now . . . I thought I heard Owen's bagpipes playing taps."

Denny shook his head. "He's left it a bit late, hasn't he?"

Callum Farthing had not enjoyed the rain-sodden, heaving journey from Banrigh to the smaller island, and he hoped that he would not have to prolong the visit any further by having to track down Owen Gilchrist. He had hauled the boat up out of the water no farther onto the stony beach than necessary not to risk its going adrift again. Through the sheets of rain he could see the orange of Owen's tent farther inland among the rocks. Oh, Christ, I'll have to help him take it down, he thought.

Cupping his hands against his cheeks, he shouted Owen's name against the wind. No one answered.

He's not out working his site in weather like this, Callum told himself. I'd have seen him. Not likely anyhow! Trust him to have found some dry little cave to hole up in, and I'll be freezing my bum off going in search of him.

He decided to look at the tent first, to see if Owen had left his tools or his food there. It might give him a better idea of where to search. His hands were even wetter now. He blew on them for warmth and thrust them into the pockets of his anorak. They'd be cold again soon enough; he'd have to use his hands for balance to clamber up the rocks to the tent. The rain made everything slick as glass.

Callum took his time negotiating the jutting rocks, losing his footing more than once and thinking what a nuisance it was going to be to carry the gear down to the boat. Perhaps they could pitch the unbreakable stuff off the rock onto the beach. He didn't fancy making half a dozen trips of it.

"Hallo! Owen!" he shouted, as he neared the tent. "Are you in there, man? I've come to fetch you."

Callum eased open one of the tent flaps, and in the shadow of the light from outside he saw Owen lying peacefully in his sleeping bag. "What a time for kipping! Have you not heard me yelling myself hoarse for you?" He reached down to shake him awake, but the shoulder was stiff to the touch. "Owen, damn you, man—"

Then he saw Owen's face, bluish in the storm's gray light. The swollen tongue pushed its way through bared teeth, and Owen's eyes stared through Callum at nothing. Callum did not know how long he had been dead. The cold eased the smell of sickness. The body would lose heat quickly here. He did not want to touch it anyway. He turned away from the ugly sight of the corpse, without any conscious thought except some vague instinct to summon help. The bagpipes lay cast off in one corner of the tent. Callum, who had been a piper in Scouts, crawled out of the tent, dragging the instrument behind him.

Outside in the cold, clean rain, he lifted the mouthpiece to his lips and played taps as hard as he could. The effort eased the tightness in his chest and emptied his lungs of the urge to scream and go on screaming.

He had no sensation of time or rain or coldness on the trip back to the larger island. His mind was filled with questions about Owen and with wondering if he had done the right thing. He was scrambling up the rocks toward the Nissen hut before he realized that the others would not have understood his signal. He had told Owen to play taps as a sign that he wanted to come back, and of course they would think that it had been an impatient Owen who had sent out the message by bagpipes. He wondered if anyone would want to see the body. If so, they could go without him.

He thought he must look like the ghost of a drowned sailor as he flung open the door of the hut and stood staring at the cozy scene inside. Four people were seated at the wooden table playing cards, with steaming cups of tea in front of them.

Elizabeth looked up and smiled. "Good!" she said. "Now I can start dinner. Where's Owen?"

Callum shrugged off his wet rain gear and left it where it fell. "He's back on the other island," he told her. "He's dead."

The others looked not at him but at each other, as if trying to decide what to make of this announcement. If anyone laughed, then it would be understood as a grisly joke. No one laughed.

Finally, Derek Marchand motioned for Callum to sit down at the table and pushed his own cup of tea in front of the young man. "Tell us exactly what has happened," he said quietly.

Callum recounted his trip over and his annoyance when Owen did not answer his shouts. He described his slippery climb up the rocks to the tent, and—in halting tones—he told them what he found inside.

"But we heard him playing the bagpipes," Denny said.

"No. That was me," Callum said. "I just . . . I was thinking about it, I suppose, and I just did it without knowing why. I suppose I thought you would understand it as a signal, but, of course, you didn't . . . I put the bagpipes back in the tent with him, and I came back."

"And you *left* him there?" Elizabeth demanded, her face pale except for two spots of color on her cheeks.

Derek Marchand nodded. "That was wise of you, Callum."

Tom Leath spoke up. "I quite agree," he said. "We've no idea what he died of. Penumonia, perhaps. Drugs, for all we know. But we must take precautions. The authorities can deal with all that when they get here in a few hours." He slid off the bench and knelt in front of the radio, now sitting on two wooden crates in the corner.

"Yes, do call for help now, Tom," said Marchand. "We seem to be having more than our share of bad luck."

Elizabeth and Denny looked at each other with raised eyebrows. Luck?

"Right," Leath said. "I won't go into too much detail on the radio. Just that there's been a suspicious death, and . . ." His voice trailed off into silence. He frowned at the radio and began adjusting knobs, but the usual crackle of static from the instrument never sounded. "What the hell . . ."

Denny went over to the radio. "Need some help?"

"The thing acts as if it were dead, but it was switched off just now. I can't understand . . . Help me get the casing off."

For several silent minutes, the two of them worked at the screws on the front of the radio. Elizabeth stared into her mug of tea, trying not to look frightened. Cameron is going to come and get me tonight, she thought to herself over and over. Derek Marchand did not seem to realize that he was drumming his fingers against the wooden table, but no one seemed to notice. Callum was staring at the wall, the tea still untouched between his hands.

Two voices swore in unison, and the others looked up sharply.

"It has been tampered with," Tom Leath said grimly. "Somebody has disconnected the wire to the off-switch, so that even when the radio is turned to the *off* position, it continues to run."

"The batteries are dead," said Denny.

"I'll get the spares," said Leath. He pulled the supply crate toward him and began to rummage inside it among the tools, boxes of chalk, rolls of film. "Where did we put the batteries?"

"In there," Denny insisted. "Let me look."

They all looked, handing the items round one at a time and even looking inside the chalk boxes. The batteries were gone. Nor were they in the food boxes or the medical kit.

"Why has somebody stranded us here on this island?" Denny wondered aloud.

Elizabeth shivered. "What if somebody is killing us off one by one?"

"Nonsense!" Marchand said. "Alasdair's fall was an accident, and we don't even know what killed young Gilchrist!''

''Hadn't we ought to try to find out?'' Denny asked.

''No!'' said Leath. ''That could be much more dangerous than not knowing. I say we get off this island as soon as possible and let the authorities sort it out.''

''We won't get far in that boat,'' Callum said. ''Not in this storm. It would take us quite a long time anyway, even in good weather. There's only one pair of oars, and navigation might be tricky.''

Leath shrugged. ''Head east. You're bound to hit land soon enough.''

Elizabeth sipped her tea with a thoughtful expression. Marchand could be right, of course. Alasdair most probably slipped and fell on his own, and Owen might have died of the flu. But the sabotaged radio told her otherwise. And if she were right about there being a connection between the deaths, then one of the people in the hut was very dangerous indeed. She wished that she could confide in Denny and ask him what he thought of it all. Surely, he was not the killer.

CHAPTER

14

On Tuesday the storm did not lessen, and the five people in the Nissen hut said very little to each other. They had lost interest in bridge. Elizabeth sat huddled at the wooden table writing in her traveler's diary, and Derek Marchand made notes about the stone circle to accompany his diagram. Leath had abandoned his earlier discretion about his private stock of alcohol, and he sat sipping straight Scotch out of his china tea mug. Even Denny seemed more subdued than usual.

"May I have some tea, Elizabeth?" Callum asked hoarsely. "I caught a chill out there last night."

"Sore throat?" she asked.

"Mostly a cough."

She nearly said that she was surprised at his asking her to fix him anything. The others had tried to be nonchalant about fixing their own food, but the unvoiced suspicion was obvious. Only Denny had eaten from anything that had already been opened; he had put marmalade on his bread. Elizabeth looked closer at Callum. He had not shaved, and he was wearing the same jeans and sweatshirt he'd slept in. She thought he looked pale and tired. The shock of the night before had not worn off. Without another word she fixed him a cup of tea.

"Elizabeth, what are the chances that Dawson will turn up in midweek?" Marchand asked, trying to sound offhand.

Elizabeth looked up from the card game she had started. "None," she said. "I asked him on Saturday, and he said he hadn't time."

"A pity," Marchand said softly. "Still, I suppose we will manage without him. Er, how is your patience coming along?"

"My what?"

Marchand pointed to the seven rows of cards spread out on the table. "Your game. We call it patience."

Elizabeth sighed. "Americans call it solitaire," she told him. "And that's the best explanation for the difference in our cultures that I have ever heard."

Leath wished that the rain would stop drumming on the tin roof. It was beginning to give him a headache. Well, perhaps the Scotch had been a contributing factor, but the rain and the tension were chiefly to blame. He had tried to read a paperback spy novel, but each time he started a new page, he realized that he had no idea what he had read on the last one.

"Farthing, will you stop coughing?" he snapped, without looking up from the page.

"How do you propose that I do that?" Callum asked wearily.

Elizabeth, now in a game of gin with Denny, touched Callum's arm. "Would you like one of Denny's pills, Callum?"

He smiled bitterly. "Denny's clap pills? That isn't what ails me, thanks. What I need is a bit of cough syrup."

"I could make you some more tea. We don't have any cough syrup, but my mother used to put honey in things when we were sick. Is Owen's jar of honey still around?"

"Thanks, I'll have my tea straight," Callum croaked. "And I think I'll have a lie-down. The light hurts my eyes, and talking makes me cough."

"He's got the flu from being out last night," Elizabeth whispered to Denny when Callum had stumbled off to a sleeping bag in a far corner of the hut. "And between this rain and the cold, we'll all have it before long."

Denny frowned. "Are you not feeling well, hen?"

"I'm fine," said Elizabeth, measuring out the tea. "But it's only a matter of time."

"They'll come and get us soon," Denny said cheerfully.

"Have you got a chance of fixing the radio, Denny?"

"Not a hope."

She looked around for inspiration. "What about using the batteries from the surveying instrument?"

Denny yawned. "I thought of that. Wrong size. Not enough power anyhow. Maybe somebody more electronically inclined could make that work, but I doubt it. Anyhow, it's beyond Leath and me, I'm afraid."

Elizabeth looked at him with troubled eyes. "I'm afraid, too," she said.

She told herself that Cameron would become worried when he tried unsuccessfully to contact them by radio. But of course he would blame that on the storm. He might think that they were cold and miserable in their damp tin hut in the middle of nowhere, but he would not consider it enough of an emergency to take him out into rough seas in his small launch. She was not even sure that she wanted such heroics from him. There had been enough tragedy already without risking the sacrifice of Cameron as well.

Leath and Marchand had put on their rain gear and announced that they were going out to have a look around. Elizabeth, feeling very much alone, was trying to read *Wuthering Heights* again, but she had reached the part where Catherine was dying, and she couldn't bear to go on with it.

Denny, who had been taking a nap in the corner, wandered over and sat beside her. "Do you think we ought to check on Callum?" he asked.

"I did. While you were asleep. He said he wasn't hungry. I suppose we ought to let him rest."

"I wish he'd do the same for us. His coughing gave me nightmares. Me being chased by the Gabriel hounds," Denny smiled. "Or maybe it's the wee folk sent me that dream, letting me know that the island is cursed."

"It certainly seems to be. First, Alasdair is hurt messing about with the babies' graves, and then Owen is working on the menhir and he dies." Elizabeth took a deep breath. What did she have to lose by talking to him? "Do you think it's a coincidence?"

Denny looked puzzled. "How do you mean? Are you saying you believe in fairy curses?"

"No, of course not! I mean, do you think somebody is making this happen?" She lowered her voice to the barest whisper. "One of us!"

He shrugged. "I can't think why anyone would."

"I know. That's had me worried all afternoon. Suppose . . . suppose Alasdair found something? I know he was taunting Owen, but suppose he wasn't kidding? If he really found treasure, and somebody wanted it . . ."

"Enough to try to kill all the rest of us?" Denny said lightly. "That would have to be quite a treasure."

"I realize that. Something on the order of Sutton Hoo."

"A Viking ship full of golden artifacts? Yes, that would do nicely. But wouldn't it look a bit odd to have all of us die on the expedition, except for one lone survivor, and then *he* suddenly purchases a castle and a Bentley? People would get suspicious."

Elizabeth nodded. "Besides, from Callum's description, Owen didn't die violently. He was just sick."

Denny smiled. "Fairy curse, I tell you. They're protecting their stone circle. And speaking of the bad luck of Banrigh, how's that finger of yours?"

She glanced at her bandage. "I ought to have had stitches," she said.

"You were the first casualty of the island, weren't you?"

"Yes." She smiled. "And I assure you that nobody sabotaged me. I was quite alone on the beach when I cut my finger. It was my own stupidity."

"Was the seal there at the time?"

Elizabeth closed her eyes and tried to remember. "He might have been."

"There you have it!" Denny smiled. "Everybody knows that seals are magic beings in disguise. He probably wants us off his island. Well, at least you've been taking the pills.

151

Modern science thwarts wee folk. It's time for another one, isn't it?''

She reached for the bottle that sat on the table beside the cup of sugar. "I suppose so. And for you, as well."

"Nag, nag, nag," said Denny. "My symptoms are quite gone away now. I think I'll cut back to one a week. I feel fine."

"What we really need is some good old American liquid cold medicine."

"Check the medical chest. Surely there's cold capsules in there. They'd be counting on somebody coming down with catarrh, what with all the wet and the cold out here."

Elizabeth set the white metal box on the table. "Bandages . . . scissors . . . iodine. Ah, what's this?" She held up a bright yellow box. "Nonprescription cold capsules. One every eight hours. Yeah, this sounds like the stuff we take at home to dry up a runny nose. As soon as Callum wakes up, I'll make him take one."

Denny frowned. "How many capsules are in there?"

"Twenty-four. No. One is missing. Twenty-three. Why?"

"I think we should all start taking them."

Leath and Marchand came back in less than an hour, stamping their wet boots in the doorway and peeling off anoraks shiny with rain. "It shows no sign of letting up, I'm afraid," Marchand said. "We went down to look at the boat."

Denny stared at them openmouthed. "You're not going to try anything in that boat?"

"It isn't very seaworthy," Marchand agreed, "but we can't be more than ten miles or so from another island."

"And if you miss it, there's always New Jersey!"

Marchand forced himself to smile. "I thought I might give it a try tomorrow. The weather should be better by then, and perhaps I shall feel more up to the task."

Elizabeth shook her head. "You should not have been tramping around in the rain like that. But never mind; Denny and I have found the cold capsules, and we are all going to take them." She waited, hands on hips, for an argument.

Marchand said gravely, "Thank you, my dear. I think that is a very good idea."

"So do I," Tom Leath said. "I'm having one now with my Scotch. Would anyone care to join me?"

About seven o'clock Elizabeth took a cold capsule to Callum, who was still sleeping. Shaking him gently awake, she put the cold capsule in his hand. "Take this," she said. "It's one of the cold capsules, and I've brought you some water. How do you feel?"

Callum's shrug turned into a cough. "The same, I guess," he said. He tossed the capsule into his mouth and gulped most of the water from the tin cup. "I hate the flu."

Elizabeth nodded. "We'll probably all get it. The rest of us took these cold capsules at dinner."

Callum looked up at her with red-rimmed eyes. "I've been trying not to think about Owen," he said. "I didn't stay long enough to get a good look at him, but . . . suppose he died of something contagious, and suppose that when I went into his tent, I caught it. . . ."

Elizabeth laughed gently. "In Britain they immunize babies against things like smallpox and diphtheria, don't they? They do in the States."

"Of course we do."

Elizabeth nodded. "I thought so. Have you had shots for typhoid?"

"Sure. As an archaeologist, of course you—"

"Tetanus?"

"Yes, but—"

"Okay, let's get really way out. Cholera?"

"Actually, yes. I took a holiday in Turkey last year."

"God, you're better off than I am," Elizabeth said. "They don't make you take cholera shots to come to Scotland. Anyhow, you see my point. You have been protected against everything we can think of. I mean, what else is there?"

He tried to smile. "Leprosy?"

"Right. That takes two to seven years' incubation, and it causes numbness. Take two aspirin and call me at the turn of the century." She relaxed a bit when he laughed. She was worried about him, and she wanted to be reassuring. She wanted them both to feel safe. It sounded logical enough. But she was still frightened.

Callum closed his eyes. "Then what killed Owen?"

Elizabeth took a deep breath. "Callum, I think he was poisoned."

"What—by one of us? That's insane."

"I've been over and over it. Nothing else makes sense. So I think we ought to be very careful."

"And not take capsules offered us by fellow diggers?"

"It isn't me!" she hissed. "And you'll need those capsules to get your strength back. Somebody has to get us off this island fast, and you're the best sailor we've got."

"What if I'm a killer?" he teased.

She patted his hand. "Then you're too sick to be dangerous, aren't you?"

Elizabeth lay huddled in her sleeping bag that night with her copy of *Wuthering Heights* and a dwindling stack of tissues beside her. She told herself that with a runny nose, she could not afford to waste her few tissues on tears. Tomorrow would be Wednesday . . . wouldn't it? Cameron was coming on Saturday. And if it kept raining so hard until then, the seas would be dry and they could walk away from the island, she thought, half-asleep. The sound of coughing kept her awake far into the night, but she finally fell into a fitful sleep sometime past three o'clock. What woke her up again a few hours later was silence. She realized that she could no longer hear the clatter of rain on the roof.

Pulling her sweater on over her T-shirt, Elizabeth eased out of the sleeping bag and crept to the door. She pushed it open a few inches and saw the graying sky of dawn. There was mist, but no downpour. She took a deep breath of sea air and stretched. No more endless days cooped up in a tin can listening to war stories and British jokes! She decided to take the bucket down to the burn. The endless cups of tea had depleted their supply of water.

Tucking the metal handle into the crook of her arm, she made her way over the rocks and down the path to the meadow. She thought that it might be nice to stay out for a while, despite the cold, and perhaps to watch the sun rise over the stone circle. She even thought of offering up a prayer from within the confines of that ancient temple. Surely it had been meant for worship of some sort; man reserved his greatest efforts for offerings to his gods. And she felt that a prayer might make her feel better, if nothing else. Or a thank-you to somebody. Because the rain had stopped, so that they could try to escape by sea and the nightmare was over.

She washed her face and hands in the cold water of the burn, glad of the stinging numbness it brought to her skin. She would heat water and have a proper wash later, but this she needed to celebrate life. She scooped water to the brim of the bucket and, after a moment's thought, let it rush back into the stream again. She could leave the bucket there and get water when she was ready to go back to the Nissen hut. No need to carry a heavy bucket all the way to the standing stones, she thought, smiling. Water would be no offering to a god of Celts!

She did not know which way the ancient builders had intended for the circle to be entered. They had created a north-south avenue of small stones leading up to the circle, but no one seemed to know what its purpose had been. Some of these small stones were still visible, half-buried in the peat. The stones themselves made her think of black-robed figures gathered around a grave. She hesitated for a few minutes before walking into the circle, feeling afraid of the place for the first time. How different it was from before! How casual they had been only a few mornings before, when everyone had come down in a pack, intent on work and chattering among themselves after a hearty breakfast. The majesty of the stones had been there even then, but it had not been so imposing. Back then, even a word could have broken the spell. Now that she was alone and frightened in the early hours of dawn, she felt as if she were expected to say something. To whom? To the stones, or to those long-ago islanders who built them? Or to the old gods themselves?

She shivered. Stop it, she thought. It is peaceful here. And the day will be fine. You are safe.

She spent a long time walking inside the circle, looking at the slant of light over the mountains from first one stone and then another, and once she tried to find an alignment with the just-visible stone on the far island, but that made her think of Owen, and she turned her back on it, determined to think of something else.

As the sky grew lighter, she began to feel warmer and more at ease, and she was leaning against the largest stone, thinking of Cameron and of spending a few days on Skye after this was over, when she heard someone calling her name.

She felt a clutch of coldness, and her first thought was that it was Owen, not dead after all, who had staggered to the menhir and was calling to her for help, but a moment later she recognized the voice. It was Denny, trotting across the meadow, shouting for her.

She didn't feel like shouting back from the circle. Somehow it would be disrespectful. She stood up, walked to the center of the circle, and waved, unsmiling.

He saw her then, and he did not smile, either. She saw that he was pale, and his hands were clenched into fists.

"What is it?" she called out even before he reached the circle. She wished she didn't have to hear—whatever it was going to be. She had never seen Denny so solemn.

"So, you're all right," he said when he reached her. He peered into her face, as if he would decide that for himself.

She nodded. "Everyone was still asleep, and I just wanted

to get out for a bit. I took the bucket to the burn, in case you were looking for it.''

"I looked there first. I thought . . . I don't know.''

She stared at him wide-eyed. "Did you think something had happened to me, Denny?''

He looked away. "Not exactly. I thought you might have taken the boat . . .''

"What? And left all of you?''

He shrugged. "I wouldn't have blamed you. I thought of it myself.'' Seeing her bewilderment, he took a deep breath and shut his eyes. "Listen, you silly git, Callum is dead. He woke up coughing and he couldn't breathe, and as I sat there trying to figure out what the hell to do about it . . . he just died.''

Elizabeth shook her head in disbelief. "He had the flu!'' she whispered.

"I don't know what he had,'' Denny said softly. "But Leath and Marchand have it, too.'' Holding his fist up to his mouth, he began to cough.

CHAPTER

15

Elizabeth followed Denny back to the burn and scooped up a bucketful of cold water. Denny knelt down on a flat rock at the water's edge and cupped a handful of water, smelling it carefully. He shrugged. "You don't think it's poisoned, do you?"

Elizabeth shook her head. "Haven't we all had typhoid shots?"

"I was thinking about some kind of manmade stuff. Arsenic or some such thing."

"I don't think you can poison a fast-flowing stream. And I wash the bucket with boiling water. Look, Denny, maybe we were just being edgy. Alasdair had an accident; Owen died of who-knows-what; and the rest of us are coming down with the flu."

"Callum was twenty-three and strong as a horse. Do you think he died of the flu?"

"Well, if one of us is a poisoner, he's an idiot. We're all

eating the same food and drinking the same water. If one of us is committing murder, I don't see how he can expect to survive."

Denny looked at her carefully. "You're not sick."

"No. But I'm terrified. I'm miserable. Denny, be reasonable. Not charitable, just reasonable. If I were going to kill anybody for fun, would Gitte have walked off this island under her own power?"

He smiled. "Good point."

"And besides, I don't think many murderers like to watch people actually die. I suppose Owen would know. I wish we could ask him . . ."

Denny stood up and brushed his wet hand against the leg of his jeans. "I suppose we ought to get back. Leath isn't bedfast or anything, but Marchand seems pretty hard hit. We have to do what we can."

"How do you feel, Denny?"

He shrugged. "Bit short of breath. Scratchy throat. It does feel like flu, now you mention it." He smiled. "I took my clap pill this morning, like a good fellow. Stupid, isn't it, to worry about a minor infection when you may be dying of something else altogether?"

"You are not dying!" Elizabeth snapped. She felt the chill again in the pit of her stomach. What would be worse? To feel herself falling sick like the rest of them, or to be the only one left healthy, and to watch them all die? Please, she thought, looking up at the bright blue sky, let the weather hold.

They took turns carrying the bucket back to the Nissen hut. All was quiet. Even the sea was silent in the August sunshine. As they neared the hut, Elizabeth shrank back, suddenly remembering what might be inside. "Is Callum still in there?" she whispered.

"Yes. I didn't know what else to do. I realize that he could contaminate us by staying, but I might also get contaminated by touching him to move him."

"I'll help you," said Elizabeth. "I think if we zipped him all the way into a sleeping bag and put him in one of the tents—that isn't too terrible, is it?"

"No. It's bloody sensible." He eased open the door and peered into the semidarkness. "Leath! We're back. How are—"

Elizabeth saw him stiffen. "What's wrong?" she demanded, thinking: *he's dead, too.*

Denny closed the door and leaned against it. "He's not there."

"I don't blame him," Elizabeth said. "I don't really want to go in there, either. I'm glad he's well enough to go out walking."

Denny grunted. "He didn't look well enough to me. Go in and make the tea, hen. I'll be back soon."

"Go in and make the tea," he'd said, making it sound so easy. The sort of task women were always assigned in times of crisis. But Elizabeth felt considerably undomestic at the prospect. She was to walk in to a dimly lit tin hut containing a corpse and a dying man—and make tea. Never mind the risk of contamination . . . never mind the horror.

She pulled open the door and went in. It couldn't be worse than labs with Milo. As a forensic anthropologist, she had done her share of work with bodies in every stage of decay. Lord, she dreaded hunting season, when the deer stalkers would stumble across an old person who had wandered away from home the spring before and died of exposure. The remains would come to the university in a green plastic body bag, waiting for the forensic anthropologists to utilize their skills and to tell them who this lump of flesh had been. It couldn't be worse than a ripe corpse from a southern forest. It was only that this time she knew the deceased personally.

"Hello, Mr. Marchand!" she said, trying to sound cheerful. "I've brought some water."

She hauled the bucket over the doorsill and carried it with two hands to the wooden table near the gas stove. She wouldn't look at the still form in the corner . . . Callum.

Derek Marchand coughed, a dry, raspy cough that went on too long. "I'll try a bit of tea," he said. He sounded out of breath as he spoke.

Elizabeth dipped some water into the red saucepan. "I'll just heat a bit right now, so that it will boil quicker. Have you had your cold capsule?"

"No. I've been dozing off, I think. Have you seen Tom?"

"Denny has gone to look for him. Now, here's your capsule. You can take it with your tea." I almost called him *ducks*, Elizabeth thought to herself. I sound like an English girl in a head scarf. For some reason this did not please her.

"We have been having some very bad luck, I'm afraid," Marchand remarked.

Elizabeth nodded, busying herself with tea things. "You must feel like Howard Carter," she remarked, thinking of the King Tut curse.

Marchand had a coughing spasm of almost a minute's duration. Without a word Elizabeth passed him a tin cup of cold water. When he could speak again, he said, as if nothing had happened, "You know, I was thinking about the Carter expedition just this morning. They picked up some sort of lung virus from the stale air in that Egyptian tomb, and it was fatal in several cases."

Elizabeth nodded. "I read about that. But we weren't doing any excavating of tombs."

Marchand looked searchingly at her. "You dug an exploratory trench, as I recall."

"But I didn't find anything!" Elizabeth protested.

"I thought not. Certainly none of us found anything like a burial chamber."

"Unless Alasdair . . ." she shrugged. Alasdair wasn't sick, only clumsy. "So you don't believe in ancient curses protecting sacred sites?"

"I am an engineer, young woman, not a guru."

Elizabeth smiled. "The tea is ready," she announced, pouring the water from the saucepan into the china mugs. Would you like to take it outside? It's a fine sunny day."

She helped him out of his sleeping bag and waited through the spasm of coughing that this provoked. "I think the sunshine will do you good," she said in a faltering voice.

Marchand cleared his throat, "Well, at any rate, it won't do me any harm."

They settled themselves on a rock in full sunshine, overlooking the sea. Elizabeth and Marchand took their cold capsules together, making it into a toast, but Elizabeth had tried to swallow both it and her antibiotic at the same time, and, before she succeeded in keeping them down, she succumbed to a fit of coughing. She was wiping the tears from her eyes and still catching her breath when Denny reappeared.

He looked at her suspiciously. "You've not got it as well?"

"No," she said. "I swallowed the wrong way. Where is Tom Leath?"

Denny frowned. "He's gone. The boat's gone as well."

Elizabeth stared. "I thought you said he was too sick!"

"So he is," Marchand said thoughtfully. "I think he must have been very frightened. Illness takes some people that way, particularly if they are not used to it. He must have felt it was a desperate chance."

"You don't think he caused all this?"

"No. Not as ill as he was. He coughed all night."

"But suppose he gets sicker out there?" Elizabeth asked.

Marchand shrugged. "Then he will die at sea."

"Meanwhile," said Denny, stifling a cough, "we are stuck here on this rock." He sank down beside Marchand. "God, I'm tired. That bit of rock climbing to the beach and back has taken the wind out of me."

Elizabeth looked thoughtfully at him. He is sicker than he lets on, she thought. And he is in no shape to do anything to help. But if something isn't done, he may die, and Derek Marchand surely will. Aloud she said, "Stay here with Marchand, Denny. You have everything you need. I'm just going to have a look around for myself."

"I tell you, Leath is gone . . ."

"Yes, I believe you. I'm looking for something else."

Denny looked scornful. "And what are you looking for?"

"I don't know."

* * *

The midmorning sun was warm. Elizabeth pulled off her navy-blue sweater and tied it around her waist. She would be warm enough in her T-shirt, she thought. She looked at her finger. She had forgotten to change the bandage that morning. Peeling the adhesive away from the cut, she looked at the red slash above the knuckle, wondering if it was too late for stitches. Still, there was no swelling, no telltale red line of blood poisoning. At least she had avoided that mishap. She wondered if a curse had been flung at her and had missed.

She took the path along the edge of the mountains that would lead to the other side of the island. Suppose the villagers had died of some disease long ago? But they hadn't. They had moved off the island a few at a time, until finally a handful of elderly folk became too tired to hold out anymore and moved away. Besides, no one had disturbed their cemetery. She couldn't even remember having seen it. As Marchand had said, no one had done any digging on the island except her, with that one exploratory trench, which was shallow and had turned up nothing.

Except Alasdair. He had been taking soil samples. She remembered noticing one such place near the hut. Fortunately, Alasdair had not been particularly neat with his sample-taking. His test areas should be easy to spot. She began to pay careful attention to the ground as she walked, looking for evidence of disturbed soil.

Why am I doing this? she asked herself. If Alasdair found anything, Alasdair would have got sick, and he didn't. That we know of, she told herself. His symptoms might have developed in the hospital, where they could find out what was wrong with him and treat him. Lucky Alasdair.

This last thought took a moment to sink in, and she nearly

stumbled on a rock in the road when its significance hit her. Very lucky Alasdair. He has an accident at the one time that there is a boat available to take him off the island. The radio is put out of order so that no one else can get off the island. And then people start to die.

At first she had thought Alasdair might have found a treasure that he wanted to conceal; but now she knew what he must have found. The question was why he would have used it, and the answer to that did not lie on the island.

CHAPTER

16

Cameron Dawson was not particularly interested in the state of the weather. He had spent much of the past few days in the laboratory monitoring blips from the radio collars of seals that had been banded earlier by other marine biologists who were still maintaining their own tracking stations on Skye and the mainland. He drank endless cups of coffee and watched his screen. It was a week of routine and monotony. The weather was all one to him, except that it had delayed the ferry that brought the mail. He had a letter from home and a newspaper still folded in front of him. He always saved his mail to read during lunch, as a distraction from his unappetizing sandwich.

Occasionally he thought of Elizabeth, whom he would be seeing in three days. They must be very busy, keeping late hours at the dig site in the long summer evenings, because he had been unable to reach them by radio. Or perhaps the rainstorm—the one that had delayed the ferry, now that he thought of it—had hampered their reception. It did not really matter, as he had no news. Alasdair had been taken to Inverness by emergency medical helicopter, accompanied by his stone-faced girlfriend, and Cameron had heard no news of him. He kept delaying his own trip to the mainland for supplies. He would have to go before Saturday, though. There were supplies he had promised to take to Banrigh, and of course they would want news of their injured friend. Cameron knew that he had an unfortunate tendency to get caught up in a project to the exclusion of everything else. Elizabeth had mentioned it often enough. He must try to spend some time with her before the end of their time in Scotland.

A break in the sound pattern in the room caught his attention. He had been switching frequencies to check on the transmissions of the radio collars of the various seals when an odd sequence made him stop. He switched back to that frequency and listened.

. It was not making the uniform sounds he had been accustomed to. The sounds were coming at regular intervals . . . intervals of varying duration. Perhaps the animal had been injured. He kept listening. There was a familiar regularity about it.

Cameron took a long gulp of black coffee. Hell! He hoped it wasn't what he first suspected. Some sailors had killed the seal and were playing games with its collar. He checked to see where the animal had been. At last monitoring it had been on shore. In fact, he thought it might be the one Elizabeth had told him she'd seen on Banrigh.

Elizabeth . . .

With half a smile he remembered what she'd said about not being able to talk intimately on a shortwave radio. So she had snatched a seal collar, silly git! Still, he was rather flattered. He hoped he could make out the message.

With pencil in hand, he began to note the sounds. One dot. Four dashes. *Four* dashes! Morse code, of course. Numbers, then. They were the easiest to remember. A one was one dot, four dashes; two was two dots, three dashes—it always added up to a sequence of five. Five was five dots, and at six the process reversed, with dashes preceding dots, so that six was the reverse of one: one dash, four dots.

Nearly half an hour later, he had narrowed the signal down to eight symbols, separated at midpoint by a long pause, as if to denote a word break.

He looked at the sheet of paper. 1-3-4-8 (long pause) 1-6-6-5. Now, what was that? He tried substituting letters, and got *A-C-D-H . . . A-F-F-E.* It made no sense. *C-D* could be his initials, but he could not find any logical meanings for *A* and *H.*

He tried the sequence backward. *H-D-C-A . . . E-F-F-A.* It wasn't English. He was pretty sure it wasn't Gaelic. And it couldn't be much of a love message, if it was *that* hard to decipher. Cameron looked at his watch. Why would Elizabeth be sending him messages in the middle of a sunny day when she ought to be working? Would she really remove a seal collar for such a frivolous reason?

He began to worry without understanding why. Was this connected to their radio silence?

He stared at the sequence again. 1-3-4-8 . . . 1-6-6-5. Suppose you took it as numbers, not letters? 1348-1665.

It made sense. But it was insane. It was a joke.

He looked again at his watch. Nobody would tap out dots and dashes with a radio transmitter for nearly an hour for a joke. They might make such an effort for a signal for help. But then, why not tap out S-O-S? That was easy enough. Everybody knew three dots, three dashes, three dots. He considered the numbers, and he thought he understood. Signaling S-O-S would not convey enough information, not if you were concerned about your rescuer.

Suddenly he knew that it was Elizabeth—and that she was in trouble. But he could not signal that he had received her message. She would have to take it on faith that he was coming. Cameron flipped off the machines and snatched up his mail as he went. He would need something to read on the long trip to the island, something to divert his mind from worry.

Just now, though, he had to scrounge up some diving gear.

CHAPTER

17

CAMERON

It seemed that for all the searching she had done, through
Scotland and through folklore, for bits and pieces of the past
. . . Thomas the Rhymer . . . Bonnie Prince Charlie . . .
that now the past had reached up out of the peat bogs and
seized her. For that is what the two numbers were: desig-
nations of the past, the *years* 1348 and 1665. Was she lucky
that I had paid attention in history class, or did she simply
assume that I would know, since it is my country we are
speaking of? Or perhaps I understood because I know her,
and those dates would be in her repertoire of folklore. The
nursery rhyme "Ring Around the Roses" came out of 1665;
it's the sort of thing she would remember. And being logical
and scientifically trained, I put the pieces together: 1348, the
first year of the great epidemic of the Black Death, and 1665,
the last terrible outbreak of plague in Britain. Taken together,
those numbers could mean only one thing: plague.

It is like her to gamble on a warning that might be misunderstood, when a simpler one would have brought certain help, but risk to the rescuer. Myself. There was more love in that message than I had thought.

Plague, she says. Be careful.

But she knows I will come for her, and because she sent the message, I know that she is at least alive.

I read the letter from my mother, my lips moving over the words, and I was unable to say what it contained when I finished it. The newspaper provided little more distraction, except for one brief article that I feel must be connected to what I will find on Banrigh.

The island sparkles in the sunshine, its green meadows just visible across the blue of the sea. I will go in on the cliff side this time. I do not have an hour to waste clambering over the mountain path, and the sea is calm. I can anchor the launch out beyond the rocks if need be. I have come prepared for that.

I have made myself ready to go ashore now, and as I look down at myself, I think that she has found her legend after all, for surely I look like a seal-man: shiny black skin covers me from head to foot, and flippers have become my appendages. I put the breathing apparatus in my mouth, adjust the air tank, and throw myself into the sea. My Celtic woman is waiting.

She must have been watching the sea from the rocks near the hut, for as I look up while I swim, I see her hurrying down the cliffs to meet me. She is wearing her tapestry skirt and the blue wool shawl from Princes Street. Surely this is not her everyday attire for the island. No, perhaps that is the point. It is the only thing she has not worn, which means that it is clean—the closest she has to *safe*.

The seal is no longer on the rocks. She has frightened him away now, this will change his daily pattern, and also in a small way the results of my study. I fight the current a bit to keep myself clear of the rocks and find myself in water shallow enough to stand in. She is on the beach now, but she does not come toward me, and I keep the mouthpiece in place. I am on the beach, but I am breathing air from the tank on my back. I cannot speak to her.

"Don't come any closer!" she calls out to me. "I'm not sick yet, but I may carry the infection." She half smiles, pleased with her own cleverness. "I see you understood my message."

I nod once and raise both hands to make a question, whatever question she wishes.

She sits down on the rock against the cliff, with fifteen feet of pebble-strewn beach between us. She has to speak much more loudly than usual, and it makes her American Southern accent much more noticeable. Or perhaps she reverts to that speech when she is distracted and afraid.

"Owen is dead, Cameron. Callum rowed over to the little island on Monday and found him. Callum died this morning. Marchand is very sick, and we are trapped here because Tom Leath took the rowboat. But he was sick, too. Did you pass him when you were coming here?"

I shake my head no.

"Denny is coughing badly, but he seems less affected than the others, and I still have the cold I had Saturday, but the deadly part seems to be the cough, and I don't have that. We found some cold capsules and made everyone take them, but it hasn't seemed to help."

I made the questioning gesture again.

173

"What is it? I don't know. It isn't typhoid or cholera. Callum had been immunized against those. And it isn't really bubonic plague, because I know the symptoms of that . . . *ring around the roses* . . No one has pustules or swollen lymph glands. I used the plague years because it was the only way I could think of to warn you about disease. My Morse code is limited to numbers, and I only learned those by osmosis when Bill was in Scouts."

I applaud her silently and nod for her to go on.

"I thought that we were being poisoned, but I couldn't think of any way to poison everyone. We've been eating tinned food for the last two days as a precaution, and it hasn't helped." She twists a strand of hair and looks pleased with herself again. "That's when I thought that maybe we were infected with something here on the island, but no one did any digging except me."

I shake my head and kneel down to pick up a handful of coarse sand.

"You're right," she says, watching the sand trickle through my gloved fingers. "Alasdair did soil sampling. I remembered that this morning, and I tried to find all the places he'd taken samples." She paused for effect. "On one of them, in one of the meadows near the village, I found quicklime!"

How to show her that I understand? I make the sign of the cross and bow my head.

"Yes, Cameron. A layer of quicklime under topsoil means a mass grave, either human or animal, but always from a contagious disease. The quicklime is to prevent the germs, or whatever, from getting into the soil and infecting crops or livestock. Archaeologists are told that if they come across quicklime in an exploratory trench, they must cover it up, and tell everyone on the site where the place is, so that it can be avoided.''

I am a biologist. She has put me on familiar ground. Now I know more than she. I mime the opening of a small bottle, swallowing a pill.

She frowns. ''I told you, the cold capsules didn't work.''

I shake my head a vigorous no and point to her bandaged finger. Again, I mime the pill-taking.

''My finger is fine. That's not important. Yes, I'm taking the pills for it, so that I can die of plague instead of tetanus.''

I pull the oxygen mask out of my mouth. ''You're not going to die at all, dear,'' I tell her, flapping awkwardly across the rocky beach with my arms outstretched. ''You have prevented yourself from getting the disease.''

We are back in the boat now. Together we hauled it into shore and got Marchand and Denny aboard. Denny is a bit shaky on his feet, but he'll be fine. Marchand may pull through with luck. I have given them all double doses of Denny's antibiotic, which is a form of penicillin that can both cure and prevent . . . anthrax. I took the same dose myself.

I decided that it would be best to leave the bodies of Callum and Owen where they are. The medical authorities will have to come to this island anyway to make their investigation and to see that the plague pit is sealed and marked. I can only hope that they will find Leath in his open boat before it is too late. We haven't time to look for him; Marchand and Denny must go to the hospital at once. I shall make Elizabeth go as well, just as a precaution.

Denny and Marchand are sleeping in the cabin, and Elizabeth is sitting on the deck with me, watching for land to appear on the horizon so that we will be safe.

"How did you know it was anthrax?" she asks suspiciously.

"That's what plague pits are in these islands. Bubonic plague didn't get here. I know a lot about anthrax, actually. Have you ever heard of Gruinard?"

She shakes her head. World War II is too recent in history to have caught her attention.

"During the War, British Intelligence took a Scottish island called Gruinard and deliberately contaminated it with anthrax. They were trying to develop something for germ warfare. It's still contaminated, after all these years. It will be for centuries, in fact, if they don't reverse the process, because anthrax is a spore-forming disease, which means that the organisms don't die. They simply hibernate there in the ground until conditions are favorable again."

"And how do you know so much about it?"

"We were afraid that seals might get it, because Gruinard is in the area they inhabit. They do get it, by the way. I was still in grad school when Hanley did that project, but I got to know quite a bit about the disease during the study, since he was one of my professors."

Elizabeth nods. "Alasdair found the plague pit, and of course he knows what it is. He knows it's still dangerous. And he decides to kill us all?"

"Yes. We'll come back to that. I want to know how he did it."

"I want to know *why*."

"He was a medical student. He'd know to scoop up the soil under the quicklime and to put it in a jar of water. After an hour, the sediment would settle to the bottom, and the water itself would contain the anthrax spores. To infect someone, you would have to put the spores in a substance that would make them grow. A sort of culture. Jam perhaps. Or honey.''

Elizabeth looks up, trembling. ''What about honey and hot wax, poured into the bag of a bagpipe?''

''Oh, God, nothing better! A damp moist place. The spores wake up. You blow into the pipe and disturb the air. You inhale it, and you have pneumonic anthrax. That explains the cough.''

Elizabeth is shaking. ''It explains everything. Callum played Owen's bagpipes after he found him dead.''

''That was stupid!'' I say without thinking. ''He was infected by that, and from then on, he breathed contagion with every word he spoke. No wonder the rest of you got it. Two days of flulike symptoms, and unless you treat it with penicillin, death comes in a matter of hours.

''So Denny's pills protected me,'' she murmured. ''And if he hadn't been so slack about taking them himself, he wouldn't be sick at all.''

''It lessened the severity for him. We can be thankful for that.''

Elizabeth takes a deep breath and rubs her eyes. ''Now can we get to the *why*?''

I get up and go into the cabin, where I have left my mail. The newspaper is still folded to the article in question. Silently I hand it to her.

PAROLED POISONER DIES IN HOSPITAL

Alasdair McEwan, better known as Alexander Evans, died in hospital at Inverness on Sunday, from

injuries sustained during a fall on the island of Banrigh.

The victim's true identity was not known until
his guardian, Dr. Philip Sinclair, came forward to
claim the body. Sinclair, who had been Evans's
prison psychiatrist, thought the young convict was
a gifted youth, and he determined to give him a
new life once he had served his sentence, even
sponsoring the boy to medical school under his new
name.

Evans was sentenced to indefinite juvenile deten-
tion at the age of fourteen for poisoning his entire
family with thallium. After . . .

Elizabeth lays the article aside. "Owen was right. How he
would have rejoiced!"

"Right?"

"Yes! The murder at the Witchery tour. That was Alasdair. The reporter was doing his story on the new lives of
convicted murderers. Alasdair couldn't afford to have that
get out. It wouldn't have done his medical career any good."

"I suppose Owen was playing detective. And he got too
close?"

"Yes. And the rest of us—perhaps he didn't know that
we'd be infected, too."

"He guessed, Elizabeth. Otherwise, why stage an accident so that he could get himself and Gitte safely away before
the contamination started?"

She looks troubled. "It was a real fall!"

"It had to be in order to be plausible. I suspect that it went
wrong. Alasdair must have meant to break an arm or even a
leg in his fall from the cliff. Instead, he hit his head—in just
the right place to kill him. Bad luck."

"Unless you consider the alternative. After this poisoning venture, there wouldn't have been another parole."

I see a dark shape ahead of us on the line of the sea. The island will be visible soon. I reach out to hold Elizabeth, and it is only when she shivers that I realize I am still in the black wet suit I wore to the beach.

She smiles up at me, still pale, though. "Seal-men only stay with their mortal lovers for seven years," she says lightly.

I smile back and pull her closer. "Seven years is a lifetime if you're a seal. Will you settle for a lifetime?"

We stand on the prow of the launch and watch Scotland rise out of the sea to meet us.

Don't miss one
Elizabeth MacPherson mystery
by
SHARYN McCRUMB

- *New York Times* bestselling author
- Edgar Award winner

Published by Ballantine Books

MacPHERSON'S LAMENT

The chilling legacy of the Civil War shocks
Elizabeth MacPherson when she ventures south
to Danville, Virginia. Her brother Bill has gotten
himself mixed up with some daughters of
Confederate veterans—old ladies who'd asked
him to sell an antebellum mansion but had
something more sinister planned. To help him,
Elizabeth has to uncover a Civil War secret that
may be the key to the ugly truth.

SICK OF SHADOWS

The very wealthy and eccentric Eileen Chandler is set to be married, but someone is willing to resort to murder to halt the impending nuptials. Eileen's beloved cousin Elizabeth MacPherson is on hand for the ceremony, and Elizabeth is not amused. No one in the wedding party is above suspicion when Elizabeth sets out to unmask the culprit.

LOVELY IN HER BONES

When the leader of her archaeological dig is murdered, forensic anthropologist Elizabeth MacPherson finds herself on the case. It takes a second mysterious death to start a cauldron of ideas bubbling in her head. And when she mixes a little modern know-how with some old-fashioned suspicions, Elizabeth comes up with a batch of answers that surprises even the experts.

THE WINDSOR KNOT

Elizabeth MacPherson has a rather hectic summer in front of her. Between finishing her doctoral thesis and planning her impending wedding, she must solve the case of a man who has died twice. And if she can accomplish all this, she might just get to have tea with Her Majesty the Queen!

MISSING SUSAN

The unsinkable Elizabeth MacPherson is on a tour of England's most famous murder sites with the cantankerous Rowan Rover, the tour guide who has been paid to murder an unsuspecting woman. No would-be assassin needs Elizabeth on his tail. And she'll be there until the end of the tour or the completion of Rowan's mission, whichever comes first.

Look for the newest Elizabeth
MacPherson mystery from

Sharyn McCrumb

IF I'D KILLED HIM
WHEN I MET HIM...

"Sharyn McCrumb is definitely a star in the New
Golden Age of mystery fiction. I look forward to
reading her for a long time to come."
—Elizabeth Peters

"Only a writer as accomplished as Sharyn
McCrumb can so skillfully marry farce and tragedy
with such rewarding results."
—*Book Page*

"Elizabeth's eighth outing has it all—a gaggle of
tidy mysteries, nonstop laughs, bumper-sticker
wisdom about the male animal, and some other,
sadder kinds of wisdom, too. Quite a banquet."
—*Kirkus Reviews*

A MAIN SELECTION OF THE
LITERARY GUILD®

SHARYN McCRUMB